They Call Me Carpenter

By

Upton Sinclair

1922

The Echo Library 2006

Published by

The Echo Library

Echo Library
131 High St.
Teddington
Middlesex TW11 8HH

www.echo-library.com

Please report serious faults in the text to complaints@echo-library.com

ISBN 1-40680-570-X

I

THE beginning of this strange adventure was my going to see a motion picture which had been made in Germany. It was three years after the end of the war, and you'd have thought that the people of Western City would have got over their war-phobias. But apparently they hadn't; anyway, there was a mob to keep anyone from getting into the theatre, and all the other mobs started from that. Before I tell about it, I must introduce Dr. Karl Henner, the well-known literary critic from Berlin, who was travelling in this country, and stopped off in Western City at that time. Dr. Henner was the cause of my going to see the picture, and if you will have a moment's patience, you will see how the ideas which he put into my head served to start me on my extraordinary adventure.

You may not know much about these cultured foreigners. Their manners are like softest velvet, so that when you talk to them, you feel as a Persian cat must feel while being stroked. They have read everything in the world; they speak with quiet certainty; and they are so old—old with memories of racial griefs stored up in their souls. I, who know myself for a member of the best clubs in Western City, and of the best college fraternity in the country—I found myself suddenly indisposed to mention that I had helped to win the battle of the Argonne. This foreign visitor asked me how I felt about the war, and I told him that it was over, and I bore no hard feelings, but of course I was glad that Prussian militarism was finished. He answered: "A painful operation, and we all hope that the patient may survive it; also we hope that the surgeon has not contracted the disease." Just as quietly as that.

Of course I asked Dr. Henner what he thought about America. His answer was that we had succeeded in producing the material means of civilization by the ton, where other nations had produced them by the pound. "We intellectuals in Europe have always been poor, by your standards over here. We have to make a very little food support a great many ideas. But you have unlimited quantities of food, and—well, we seek for the ideas, and we judge by analogy they must exist—"

"But you don't find them?" I laughed.

"Well," said he, "I have come to seek them."

This talk occurred while we were strolling down our Broadway, in Western City, one bright afternoon in the late fall of 1921. We talked about the picture which Dr. Henner had recommended to me, and which we were now going to see. It was called "The Cabinet of Dr. Caligari," and was a "futurist" production, a strange, weird freak of the cinema art, supposed to be the nightmare of a madman. "Being an American," said Dr. Henner, "you will find yourself asking, 'What good does such a picture do?' You will have the idea that every work of art must serve some moral purpose." After a pause, he added: "This picture could not possibly have been produced in America. For one thing, nearly all the characters are thin." He said it with the flicker of a smile—"One does not find American screen actors in that condition. Do your people care enough about the life of art to take a risk of starving for it?"

Now, as a matter of fact, we had at that time several millions of people out of work in America, and many of them starving. There must be some intellectuals among them, I suggested; and the critic replied: "They must have starved for so long that they have got used to it, and can enjoy it—or at any rate can enjoy turning it into art. Is not that the final test of great art, that it has been smelted in the fires of suffering? All the great spiritual movements of humanity began in that way; take primitive Christianity, for example. But you Americans have taken Christ, the carpenter—"

I laughed. It happened that at this moment we were passing St. Bartholomew's Church, a great brown-stone structure standing at the corner of the park. I waved my hand towards it. "In there," I said, "over the altar, you may see Christ, the carpenter, dressed up in exquisite robes of white and amethyst, set up as a stained glass window ornament. But if you'll stop and think, you'll realize it wasn't we Americans who began that!"

"No," said the other, returning my laugh, "but I think it was you who finished him up as a symbol of elegance, a divinity of the respectable inane."

Thus chatting, we turned the corner, and came in sight of our goal, the Excelsior Theatre. And there was the mob!

II

AT first, when I saw the mass of people, I thought it was the usual picture crowd. I said, with a smile, "Can it be that the American people are not so dead to art after all?" But then I observed that the crowd seemed to be swaying this way and that; also there seemed to be a great many men in army uniforms. "Hello!" I exclaimed. "A row?"

There was a clamor of shouting; the army men seemed to be pulling and pushing the civilians. When we got nearer, I asked of a bystander, "What's up?" The answer was: "They don't want 'em to go in to see the picture."

"Why not?"

"It's German. Hun propaganda!"

Now you must understand, I had helped to win a war, and no man gets over such an experience at once. I had a flash of suspicion, and glanced at my companion, the cultured literary critic from Berlin. Could it possibly be that this smooth-spoken gentleman was playing a trick upon me—trying, possibly, to get something into my crude American mind without my realizing what was happening? But I remembered his detailed account of the production, the very essence of "art for art's sake." I decided that the war was three years over, and I was competent to do my own thinking.

Dr. Henner spoke first. "I think," he said, "it might be wiser if I did not try to go in there."

"Absurd!" I cried. "I'm not going to be dictated to by a bunch of imbeciles!"

"No," said the other, "you are an American, and don't have to be. But I am a German, and I must learn."

I noted the flash of bitterness, but did not resent it. "That's all nonsense, Dr. Henner!" I argued. "You are my guest, and I won't—"

"Listen, my friend," said the other. "You can doubtless get by without trouble; but I would surely rouse their anger, and I have no mind to be beaten for nothing. I have seen the picture several times, and can talk about it with you just as well."

"You make me ashamed of myself," I cried—"and of my country!"

"No, no! It is what you should expect. It is what I had in mind when I spoke of the surgeon contracting the disease. We German intellectuals know what war means; we are used to things like this." Suddenly he put out his hand. "Goodbye."

"I will go with you!" I exclaimed. But he protested—that would embarrass him greatly. I would please to stay, and see the picture; he would be interested later on to hear my opinion of it. And abruptly he turned, and walked off, leaving me hesitating and angry.

At last I started towards the entrance of the theatre. One of the men in uniform barred my way. "No admittance here!"

"But why not?"

"It's a German show, and we aint a-goin' to allow it."

"Now see here, buddy," I countered, none too good-naturedly, "I haven't got my uniform on, but I've as good a right to it as you; I was all through the Argonne."

"Well, what do you want to see Hun propaganda for?"

"Maybe I want to see what it's like."

"Well, you can't go in; we're here to shut up this show!"

I had stepped to one side as I spoke, and he caught me by the arm. I thought there had been talk enough, and gave a sudden lurch, and tore my arm free. "Hold on here!" he shouted, and tried to stop me again; but I sprang through the crowd towards the box-office. There were more than a hundred civilians in or about the lobby, and not more than twenty or thirty ex-service men maintaining the blockade; so a few got by, and I was one of the lucky ones. I bought my ticket, and entered the theatre. To the man at the door I said: "Who started this?"

"I don't know, sir. It's just landed on us, and we haven't had time to find out."

"Is the picture German propaganda?"

"Nothing like that at all, sir. They say they won't let us show German pictures, because they're so much cheaper; they'll put American-made pictures out of business, and it's unfair competition."

"Oh!" I exclaimed, and light began to dawn. I recalled Dr. Henner's remark about producing a great many ideas out of a very little food; assuredly, the American picture industry had cause to fear competition of that sort! I thought of old "T-S," as the screen people call him for short—the king of the movie world, with his roll of fat hanging over his collar, and his two or three extra chins! I though of Mary Magna, million dollar queen of the pictures, contriving diets and exercises for herself, and weighing with fear and trembling every day!

III

IT was time for the picture to begin, so I smoothed my coat, and went to a seat, and was one of perhaps two dozen spectators before whom "The Cabinet of Dr. Caligari" received its first public showing in Western City. The story had to do with a series of murders; we saw them traced by a young man, and fastened bit by bit upon an old magician and doctor. As the drama neared its climax, we discovered this doctor to be the head of an asylum for the insane, and the young man to be one of the inmates; so in the end the series of adventures was revealed to us as the imaginings of a madman about his physician and keepers. The settings and scenery were in the style of "futurist" art—weird and highly effective. I saw it all in the light of Dr. Henner's interpretation, the product of an old, perhaps an overripe culture. Certainly no such picture could have been produced in America! If I had to choose between this and the luxurious sex-stuff of Mary Magna—well, I wondered. At least, I had been interested in every moment of "Dr. Caligari," and I was only interested in Mary off the screen. Several times every year I had to choose between mortally hurting her feelings, and watching her elaborate "vamping" through eight or ten costly reels.

I had read many stories and seen a great many plays, in which the hero wakes up in the end, and we realize that we have been watching a dream. I remembered "Midsummer Night's Dream," and also "Looking Backward." An old, old device of art; and yet always effective, one of the most effective! But this was the first time I had ever been taken into the dreams of a lunatic. Yes, it was interesting, there was no denying it; grisly stuff, but alive, and marvelously well acted. How Edgar Allen Poe would have revelled in it! So thinking, I walked towards the exit of the theatre, and a swinging door gave way—and upon my ear broke a clamor that might have come direct from the inside of Dr. Caligari's asylum. "Ya, ya. Boo, boo! German propaganda! Pay your money to the Huns! For shame on you! Leave your own people to starve, and send your cash to the enemy."

I stopped still, and whispered to myself, "My God!" During all the time—an hour or more—that I had been away on the wings of imagination, these poor boobs had been howling and whooping outside the theatre, keeping the crowds away, and incidentally working themselves into a fury! For a moment I thought I would go out and reason with them; they were mistaken in the idea that there was anything about the war, anything against America in the picture. But I realized that they were beyond reason. There was nothing to do but go my way and let them rave.

But quickly I saw that this was not going to be so easy as I had fancied. Right in front of the entrance stood the big fellow who had caught my arm; and as I came toward him I saw that he had me marked. He pointed a finger into my face, shouting in a fog-horn voice: "There's a traitor! Says he was in the service, and now he's backing the Huns!"

I tried to have nothing to do with him, but he got me by the arm, and others were around me. "Yein, yein, yein!" they shouted into my ear; and as I tried to make my way through, they began to hustle me. "I'll shove your face in, you damned Hun!"—a continual string of such abuse; and I had been in the service, and seen fighting!

I never tried harder to avoid trouble; I wanted to get away, but that big fellow stuck his feet between mine and tripped me, he lunged and shoved me into the gutter, and so, of course, I made to hit him. But they had me helpless; I had no more than clenched my fist and drawn back my arm, when I received a violent blow on the side of my jaw. I never knew what hit me, a fist or a weapon. I only felt the crash, and a sensation of reeling, and a series of blows and kicks like a storm about me.

I ask you to believe that I did not run away in the Argonne. I did my job, and got my wound, and my honorable record. But there I had a fighting chance, and here I had none; and maybe I was dazed, and it was the instinctive reaction of my tormented body—anyhow, I ran. I staggered along, with the blows and kicks to keep me moving. And then I saw half a dozen broad steps, and a big open doorway; I fled that way, and found myself in a dark, cool place, reeling like a drunken man, but no longer beaten, and apparently no longer pursued. I was falling, and there was something nearby, and I caught at it, and sank down upon a sort of wooden bench.

IV

I had run into St. Bartholomew's Church; and when I came to—I fear I cut a pitiful figure, but I have to tell the truth—I was crying. I don't think the pain of my head and face had anything to do with it, I think it was rage and humiliation; my sense of outrage, that I, who had helped to win a war, should have been made to run from a gang of cowardly rowdies. Anyhow, here I was, sunk down in a pew of the church, sobbing as if my heart was broken.

At last I raised my head, and holding on to the pew in front, looked about me. The church was apparently deserted. There were dark vistas; and directly in front of me a gleaming altar, and high over it a stained glass window, with the afternoon sun shining through. You know, of course, the sort of figures they have in those windows; a man in long robes, white, with purple and gold; with a brown beard, and a gentle, sad face, and a halo of light about the head. I was staring at the figure, and at the same time choking with rage and pain, but clenching my hands, and making up my mind to go out and follow those brutes, and get that big one alone and pound his face to a jelly. And here begins the strange part of my adventure; suddenly that shining figure stretched out its two arms to me, as if imploring me not to think those vengeful thoughts!

I knew, of course, what it meant; I had just seen a play about delirium, and had got a whack on the head, and now I was delirious myself. I thought I must be badly hurt; I bowed my reeling head in my arms, and began to sob like a kid, out loud, and without shame. But somehow I forgot about the big brute, and his face that I wanted to pound; instead, I was ashamed and bewildered, a queer hysterical state with a half dozen emotions mixed up. The Caligari story was in it, and the lunatic asylum; I've got a cracked skull, I thought, and my mind will never get right again! I sat, huddled and shuddering; until suddenly I felt a quiet hand on my shoulder, and heard a gentle voice saying: "Don't be afraid. It is I."

Now, I shall waste no time telling you how amazed I was. It was a long time before I could believe what was happening to me; I thought I was clean off my head. I lifted my eyes, and there, in the aisle of the most decorous church of St. Bartholomew, standing with his hand on my head, was the figure out of the stained glass window! I looked at him twice, and then I looked at the window. Where the figure had been was a great big hole with the sun shining through!

We know the power of suggestion, and especially when one taps the deeps of the unconscious, where our childhood memories are buried. I had been brought up in a religious family, and so it seemed quite natural to me that while that hand lay on my head, the throbbing and whirling should cease, and likewise the fear. I became perfectly quiet, and content to sit under the friendly spell. "Why were you crying?" asked the voice, at last.

I answered, hesitatingly, "I think it was humiliation."

"Is it something you have done?"

"No. Something that was done to me."

"But how can a man be humiliated by the act of another?"

I saw what he meant; and I was not humiliated any more.

The stranger spoke again. "A mob," he said, "is a blind thing, worse than madness. It is the beast in man running away with his master."

I thought to myself: how can he know what has happened to me? But then I reflected, perhaps he saw them drive me into the church! I found myself with a sudden, queer impulse to apologize for those soldier boys. "We had some terrible fighting," I cried. "And you know what wars do—to the minds of the people, I mean."

"Yes," said the stranger, "I know, only too well."

I had meant to explain this mob; but somehow, I decided that I could not. How could I make him understand moving picture shows, and German competition, and ex-service men out of jobs? There was a pause, and he asked, "Can you stand up?"

I tried and found that I could. I felt the side of my jaw, and it hurt, but somehow the pain seemed apart from myself. I could see clearly and steadily; there were only two things wrong that I could find—first, this stranger standing by my side, and second, that hole in the window, where I had seen him standing so many Sunday mornings!

"Are you going out now?" he asked. As I hesitated, he added, tactfully, "Perhaps you would let me go with you?"

Here was indeed a startling proposition! His costume, his long hair—there were many things about him not adapted to Broadway at five o'clock in the afternoon! But what could I say? It would be rude to call attention to his peculiarities. All I could manage was to stammer: "I thought you belonged in the church."

"Do I?" he replied, with a puzzled look. "I'm not sure. I have been wondering—am I really needed here? And am I not more needed in the world?"

"Well," said I, "there's one thing certain." I pointed up to the window. "That hole is conspicuous."

"Yes, that is true."

"And if it should rain, the altar would be ruined. The Reverend Dr. Lettuce-Spray would be dreadfully distressed. That altar cloth was left to the church in the will of Mrs. Elvina de Wiggs, and God knows how many thousands of dollars it cost."

"I suppose that wouldn't do," said the stranger. "Let us see if we can't find something to put there."

He started up the aisle, and through the chancel. I followed, and we came into the vestry-room, and there on the wall I noticed a full length, life-sized portrait of old Algernon de Wiggs, president of the Empire National Bank, and of the Western City Chamber of Commerce. "Let us see if he would fill the place," said the stranger; and to my amazement he drew up a chair, and took down the huge picture, and carried it, seemingly without effort, into the church.

He stepped upon the altar, and lifted the portrait in front of the window. How he got it to stay there I am not sure—I was too much taken aback by the procedure to notice such details. There the picture was; it seemed to fit the window exactly, and the effect was simply colossal. You'd have to know old de

Wiggs to appreciate it—those round, puffy cheeks, with the afternoon sun behind them, making them shine like two enormous Jonathan apples! Our leading banker was clad in decorous black, as always on Sunday mornings, but in one place the sun penetrated his form—at one side of his chest. My curiosity got the better of me; I could not restrain the question, "What is that golden light?"

Said the stranger: "I think that is his heart."

"But that can't be!" I argued. "The light is on his right side; and it seems to have an oblong shape—exactly as if it were his wallet."

Said the other: "Where the treasure is, there will the heart be also."

VI

WE passed out through the arched doorway, and Broadway was before us. I had another thrill of distress—a vision of myself walking down this crowded street with this extraordinary looking personage. The crowds would stare at us, the street urchins would swarm about us, until we blocked the traffic and the police ran us in! So I thought, as we descended the steps and started; but my fear passed, for we walked and no one followed us—hardly did anyone even turn his eyes after us.

I realized in a little while how this could be. The pleasant climate of Western City brings strange visitors to dwell here; we have Hindoo swamis in yellow silk, and a Theosophist college on a hill-top, and people who take up with "nature," and go about with sandals and bare legs, and a mane of hair over their shoulders. I pass them on the street now and then—one of them carries a shepherd's crook! I remember how, a few years ago, my Aunt Caroline, rambling around looking for something to satisfy her emotions, took up with these queer ideas, and there came to her front door, to the infinite bewilderment of the butler, a mild-eyed prophet in pastoral robes, and with a little newspaper bundle in his hand. This, spread out before my aunt, proved to contain three carrots and two onions, carefully washed, and shining; they were the kindly fruits of the earth, and of the prophet's own labor, and my old auntie was deeply touched, because it appeared that this visitor was a seer, the sole composer of a mighty tome which is to be found in the public library, and is known as the "Eternal Bible."

So here I was, strolling along quite as a matter of course with my strange acquaintance. I saw that he was looking about, and I prepared for questions, and wondered what they would be. I thought that he must naturally be struck by such wonders as automobiles and crowded street-cars. I failed to realize that he would be thinking about the souls of the people.

Said he, at last: "This is a large city?"

"About half a million."

"And what quarter are we in?"

"The shopping district."

"Is it a segregated district?"

"Segregated? In what way?"

"Apparently there are only courtesans."

I could not help laughing. "You are misled by the peculiarities of our feminine fashions—details with which you are naturally not familiar—"

"Oh, quite the contrary," said he, "I am only too familiar with them. In childhood I learned the words of the prophet: 'Because the daughters of Zion are haughty, and walk with stretched forth necks and wanton eyes, walking and mincing as they go, and making a tinkling with their feet; therefore the Lord will smite with a scab the crown of the head of the daughters of Zion, and the Lord will discover their secret parts. In that day the Lord will take away the bravery of their tinkling ornaments about their feet, and their cauls, and their round tires like the moon, the chains, and the bracelets, and the mufflers, the bonnets, and the ornaments of the legs, and the headbands, and the tablets, and the earrings, and nose jewels, the changeable suits of apparel, and the mantles, and the wimples, and the crisping pins, the glasses, and the fine linen, and the hoods, and the veils. And it shall come to pass that instead of sweet smell there shall be stink; and instead of a girdle a rent; and instead of well set hair, baldness; and instead of a stomacher a girding of sackcloth; and burning instead of beauty.'"

From the point of view of literature this might be great stuff; but on the corner of Broadway and Fifth Street at the crowded hours it was unusual, to say the least. My companion was entering into the spirit of it in a most alarming way; he was half chanting, his voice rising, his face lighting up. "'Thy men shall fall by the sword, and thy mighty in the war. And her gates shall lament and mourn; and she being desolate shall sit upon the ground.'"

"Be careful!" I whispered. "People will hear you!"

"But why should they not?" He turned on me a look of surprise. "The people hear me gladly." And he added: "The common people."

Here was an aspect of my adventure which had not occurred to me before. "My God!" I thought. "If he takes to preaching on street corners!" I realized in a flash—it was exactly what he would be up to! A panic seized me; I couldn't stand that; I'd have to cut and run!

I began to speak quickly. "We must get across this street while we have time; the traffic officer has turned the right way now." And I began explaining our remarkable system of traffic handling.

But he stopped me in the middle. "Why do we wish to cross the street, when we have no place to go?"

"I have a place I wish to take you to," I said; "a friend I want you to meet. Let us cross. "And while I was guiding him between the automobiles, I was desperately trying to think how to back up my lie. Who was there that would receive this incredible stranger, and put him up for the night, and get him into proper clothes, and keep him off the soap-box?

Truly, I was in an extraordinary position! What had I done to get this stranger wished onto me? And how long was he going to stay with me? I found myself recalling the plight of Mary who had a little lamb!

Fate had me in its hands, and did not mean to consult me. We had gone less than a block further when I heard a voice, "Hello! Billy!" I turned. Oh, Lord! Oh, Lord! Of all the thankless encounters—Edgerton Rosythe, moving picture critic of the Western City "Times." Precisely the most cynical, the most profane, the most boisterous person in a cynical and profane and boisterous business! And he had me here, in full daylight, with a figure just out of a stained glass window in St. Bartholomew's Church!

VII

"Hello, Billy! Who's your good-looking friend?" Rosythe was in full sail before a breeze of his own making.

How could I answer. "Why—er—"

The stranger spoke. "They call me Carpenter."

"Ah!" said the critic. "Mr. Carpenter, delighted to meet you." He gave the stranger a hearty grip of the hand. "Are you on location?"

"Location?" said the other; and Rosythe shot an arrow of laughter towards me. Perhaps he knew about the vagaries of my Aunt Caroline; anyhow, he would have a fantastic tale to tell about me, and was going to exploit it to the limit!

I made a pitiful attempt to protect my dignity. "Mr. Carpenter has just arrived," I began—

"Just arrived, hey?" said the critic. "Oviparous, viviparous, or oviviparous?" He raised his hand; actually, in the glory of his wit, he was going to clap the stranger on the shoulder!

But his hand stayed in the air. Such a look as came on Carpenter's face! "Hush!" he commanded. "Be silent!" And then: "Any man will join in laughter; but who will join in disease?"

"Hey?" said Rosythe; and it was my turn to grin.

"Mr. Carpenter has just done me a great service," I explained. "I got badly mauled in the mob—"

"Oh!" cried the other. "At the Excelsior Theatre!" Here was something to talk about, to cover his bewilderment. "So you were in it! I was watching them just now."

"Are they still at it?"

"Sure thing!"

"A fine set of boobs," I began—

"Boobs, nothing!" broke in the other. "What do you suppose they're doing?"

"Saving us from Hun propaganda, so they told me."

"The hell of a lot they care about Hun propaganda! They are earning five dollars a head."

"What?"

"Sure as you're born!"

"You really know that?"

"Know it? Pete Dailey was at a meeting of the Motion Picture Directors' Association last night, and it was arranged to put up the money and hire them. They're a lot of studio bums, doing a real mob scene on a real location!"

"Well, I'll be damned!" I said. "And what about the police?"

"Police?" laughed the critic. "Would you expect the police to work free when the soldiers are paid? Why, Jesus Christ——"

"I beg pardon?" said Carpenter.

"Why—er—" said Rosythe; and stopped, completely bluffed.

"You ought not swear," I remarked, gravely; and then, "I must explain. I got pounded by that mob; I was knocked quite silly, and this gentleman found me, and healed me in a wonderful way."

"Oh!" said the critic, with genuine interest. "Mind cure, hey? What line?"

I was about to reply, but Carpenter, it appeared, was able to take care of himself. "The line of love," he answered, gently.

"See here, Rosythe," I broke in, "I can't stand on the street. I'm beginning to feel seedy again. I think I'll have a taxi."

"No," said the critic. "Come with me. I'm on the way to pick up the missus. Right around the corner—a fine place to rest." And without further ado he took me by the arm and led me along. He was a good-hearted chap inside; his rowdyisms were just the weapons of his profession. We went into an office building, and entered an elevator. I did not know the building, or the offices we came to. Rosythe pushed open a door, and I saw before me a spacious parlor, with birds of paradise of the female sex lounging in upholstered chairs. I was led to a vast plush sofa, and sank into it with a sigh of relief.

The stranger stood beside me, and put his hand on my head once more. It was truly a miracle, how the whirling and roaring ceased, and peace came back to me; it must have shown in my face, for the moving picture critic of the Western City "Times" stood watching me with a quizzical smile playing over his face. I could read his thoughts, as well as if he had uttered them: "Regular Svengali stuff, by God!"

VIII

I was so comfortable there, I did not care what happened. I closed my eyes for a while; then I opened them and gazed lazily about the place. I noted that all the birds of paradise were watching Carpenter. With one accord their heads had turned, and their eyes were riveted upon him. I found myself thinking. "This man will make a hit with the ladies!" Like the swamis, with their soft brown skins, and their large, dark, cow-like eyes!

There had been silence in the place. But suddenly we all heard a moan; I felt Carpenter start, and his hand left my head. A dozen doors gave into this big parlor—all of them closed. We perceived that the sound came through the door nearest to us. "What is it?" I asked, of Rosythe.

"God knows," said he; "you never can tell, in this place of torment."

I was about to ask, "What sort of place is it?" But the moan came again, louder, more long drawn out: "O-o-o-o-o-o-o-o-oh!" It ended in a sort of explosion, as if the maker of it had burst.

Carpenter turned, and took two steps towards the door; then he stopped, hesitating. My eyes followed him, and then turned to the critic, who was watching Carpenter, with a broad grin on his face. Evidently Rosythe was going to have some fun, and get his revenge!

The sound came again—louder, more harrowing. It came at regular intervals, and each time with the explosion at the end. I watched Carpenter, and he was like a high-spirited horse that hears the cracking of a whip over his head. The creature becomes more restless, he starts more quickly and jumps farther at each sound. But he is puzzled; he does not know what these lashes mean, or which way he ought to run.

Carpenter looked from one to another of us, searching our faces. He looked at the birds of paradise in the lounging chairs. Not one of them moved a muscle—save only those muscles which caused their eyes to follow him. It was no concern of theirs, this agony, whatever it was. Yet, plainly, it was the sound of a woman in torment: "O-o-o-o-o-o-o-o-oh!"

Carpenter wanted to open that door. His hand would start towards it; then he would turn away. Between the two impulses he was presently pacing the room; and since there was no one who appeared to have any interest in what he might say, he began muttering to himself. I would catch a phrase: "The fate of woman!" And again: "The price of life!" I would hear the terrible, explosive wail: "O-o-o-o-o-o-o-o-oh!" And it would wring a cry out of the depths of Carpenter's soul: "Oh, have mercy!"

In the beginning, the moving picture critic of the Western City "Times" had made some effort to restrain his amusement. But as this performance went on, his face became one enormous, wide-spreading grin; and you can understand, that made him seem quite devilish. I saw that Carpenter was more and more goaded by it. He would look at Rosythe, and then he would turn away in aversion. But at last he made an effort to conquer his feelings, and went up to the critic, and said, gently: "My friend: for every man who lives on earth, some woman has paid the price of life."

"The price of life?" repeated the critic, puzzled.

Carpenter waved his hand towards the door. "We confront this everlasting mystery, this everlasting terror; and it is not becoming that you should mock."

The grin faded from the other's face. His brows wrinkled, and he said: "I don't get you, friend. What can a man do?"

"At least he can bow his heart; he can pay his tribute to womanhood."

"You're too much for me," responded Rosythe. "The imbeciles choose to go through with it; it's their own choice."

Said Carpenter: "You have never thought of it as the choice of God?"

"Holy smoke!" exclaimed the critic. "I sure never did!"

At that moment one of the doors was opened. Rosythe turned his eyes. "Ah, Madame Planchet!" he cried. "Come tell us about it!"

IX

A stoutish woman out of a Paris fashion-plate came trotting across the room, smiling in welcome: "Meester Rosythe!" She had black earrings flapping from each ear, and her face was white, with a streak of scarlet for lips. She took the critic by his two hands, and the critic, laughing, said: "Respondez, Madame! Does God bring the ladies to this place?"

"Ah, surely, Meester Rosythe! The god of beautee, he breengs them to us! And the leetle god with the golden arrow, the rosy cheeks and the leetle dimple—the dimple that we make heem for two hundred dollars a piece—eh, Meester Rosythe? He breengs the ladies to us!"

The critic turned. "Madame Planchet, permit me to introduce Mr. Carpenter. He is a man of wonder, he heals pain, and does it by means of love."

"Oh, how eenteresting! But what eef love heemself ees pain—who shall heal that, eh, Meester Carpentair?"

"O-o-o-o-o-o-o-h!" came the moan.

Said Rosythe: "Mr. Carpenter thinks you make the ladies suffer too much. It worries him."

"Ah, but the ladies do not mind! Pain? What ees eet? The lady who makes the groans, she cannot move, and so she ees unhappy. Also, she likes to have her own way, she ees a leetle—what you say?—spoilt. But her troubles weel pass; she weel be beautiful, and her husband weel love her more, and she weel be happy."

"O-o-o-o-o-o-o-o-oh!" from the other room; and Madame Planchet prattled away: "I say to them, Make plenty of noises! Eet helps! No one weel be afraid, for all here are worshippers of the god of beautee—all weel bear the pains that he requires. Eh, Meester Carpentair?"

Carpenter was staring at her. I had not before seen such intensity of concentration on his face. He was trying to understand this situation, so beyond all believing.

"I weel tell you something," said Madame Planchet, lowering her voice confidentially. "The lady what you hear—that ees Meeses T-S. You know Meester T-S, the magnate of the peectures?"

Carpenter did not say whether he knew or not.

"They come to me always, the peecture people; to me. the magician, the deputee of the god of beautee. Polly Pretty, she comes, and Dolly Dimple, she comes, and Lucy Love, she comes, and Betty Belle Bird. They come to me for the hair, and for the eyes, and for the complexion. You are a workair of miracles yourself—but can you do what I do? Can you make the skeen all new? Can you make the old young?"

"O-o-o-o-o-o-o-o-oh!"

"Mary Magna, she comes to me, and she breengs me her old grandmother, and she says, 'Madame,' she says, 'make her new from the waist up, for you can nevair tell how the fashions weel change, and what she weel need to show.' Ha, ha, ha, she ees wittee, ees the lovely Mary! And I take the old lady, and her wrinkles weel be gone, and her skeen weel be soft like a leetle baby's, and in her cheeks weel be two lovely dimples, and she weel dance with the young boys, and they weel not know her from her grandchild—ha, ha, ha!—ees eet not the wondair?"

I knew by now where I was. I had heard many times of Madame Planchet's beauty-parlors. I sat, wondering; should I take Carpenter by the arm, and lead him gently out? Or should I leave him to fight his own. fight with modern civilization?

"O-o-o-o-o-o-o-o-oh!"

Madame turned suddenly upon me. "I know you, Meester Billee," she said. "I have seen you with Mees Magna! Ah, naughtee boy! You have the soft, fine hair—you should let it grow—eight inches we have to have, and then you can come to me for the permanent wave. So many young men come to me for the permanent wave! You know eet? Meester Carpentair, you see, he has let hees hair grow, and he has the permanent wave—eet could not be bettair eef I had done eet myself. I say always, 'My work ees bettair than nature, I tell nature by the eemperfections.' Eh, voila?"

I am not sure whether it was for the benefit of me or of Carpenter. The deputee of the god of beautee was moved to volunteer a great revelation. "Would you like to see how we make eet—the permanent wave? I weel show you Messes T-S. But you must not speak—she would not like eet if I showed her to gentlemen. But her back ees turned and she cannot move. We do not let them see the apparatus, because eet ees rather frightful, eet would make them seek. You will be very steel, eh?"

"Mum's the word, Madame," said Rosythe, speaking for the three of us.

"O-o-o-o-o-o-o-o-oh!" moaned the voice.

"First, I weel tell you," said Madame. "For the complete wave we wind the hair in tight leetle coils on many rods. Eet ees very delicate operations—every hair must be just so, not one crooked, not one must we skeep. Eet takes a long time—two hours for the long hair; and eet hurts, because we must pull eet so tight. We wrap each coil een damp cloths, and we put them een the contacts, and we turn on the eelectreeceetee—and then eet ees many hours that the hair ees baked, ees cooked een the proper curves, eh? Now, very steel, eef you please!"

And softly she opened the door.

X

BEFORE us loomed what I can only describe as a mountain of red female flesh. This flesh-mountain had once apparently been slightly covered by embroidered silk lingerie, but this was now soaked in moisture and reduced to the texture of wet tissue paper. The top of the flesh-mountain ended in an amazing spectacle. It appeared as if the head had no hair whatever; but starting from the bare scalp was an extraordinary number of thin rods, six inches or so in length. These rods stood out in every direction, and being of gleaming metal, they gave to the head the aspect of some bright Phoebus Apollo, known as the "far-darter;" or shall I say some fierce Maenad with electric snakes having nickel-plated skins; or shall I say some terrific modern war-god, pouring poison gases from a forest of chemical tubes? Over the top of the flesh-mountain was a big metal object, a shining concave dome with which all the tubes connected; so that a stranger to the procedure could not have felt sure whether the mountain was holding up the dome, or was dangling from it. A piece of symbolism done by a maniac artist, whose meaning no one could fathom!

From the dome there was given heat; so from the pores of the flesh-mountain came perspiration. I could not say that I actually saw perspiration flowing from any particular pore; it is my understanding that pores are small, and do not squirt visible jets. What I could say is that I saw little trickles uniting to form brooks, and brooks to form rivers, which ran down the sides of the flesh-mountain, and mingled in an ocean on the floor.

Also I observed that flesh-mountains when exposed to heat do not stand up of their own consistency, but have a tendency to melt and flatten; it was necessary that this bulk should be supported, so there were three attendants, one securely braced under each armpit, and the third with a more precarious grip under the mountain's chin. Every thirty seconds or so the heaving, sliding mass would emit one of those explosive groans: "O-o-o-o-o-oh!" Then it would collapse, an avalanche would threaten to slide, and the living caryatids would shove and struggle.

Said Madame Planchet, in her stage-whisper: "The serveece of the young god of beautee!" And my fancy took flight. I saw proud vestals tending sacred flames on temple-clad islands in blue Grecian seas; I saw acolytes waving censers, and grave, bearded priests walking in processions crowned with myrtle-wreaths. I wondered if ever since the world began, the young god of beautee looking down from his crystal throne had beheld a stranger ritual of adoration!

Silently we drew back from the door-way, and Madame closed the door, reducing the promethean groans and the strong ammoniacal odors. I did not see the face of Carpenter, because he had turned it from us. Rosythe favored me with a smile, and whispered, "Your friend doesn't care for beautee!" Then he added, "What do you suppose he meant by that stuff about 'the price of life' and 'the choice of God?'"

"Didn't you really get it?" I asked.

"I'm damned if I did."

"My dear fellow," I said, "you didn't tell us what sort of place this was; and Carpenter thought it must be a maternity-ward."

The moving picture critic of the Western City "Times" gave me one wild look; then from his throat there came a sound like the sudden bleat of a young sheep in pain. It caused Carpenter to start, and Madame Planchet to start, and for the first time since we entered the place, the birds of paradise gave signs of life elsewhere than in the eye-muscles. The sheep gave a second bleat, and then a third, and Rosythe, red in the face and apparently choking, turned and fled to the corridor.

Madame Planchet drew me apart and said: "Meester Billee, tell me something. Ees eet true that thees gentleman ees a healer? He takes away the pains?"

"He did it for me," I answered.

"He ees vairy handsome, eh, Meester Billee?"

"Yes, that is true."

"I have an idea; eet ees a wondair." She turned to my friend. "Meester Carpentair, they tell me that you heal the pains. I think eet would be a vairy fine thing eef you would come to my parlor and attend the ladies while I give them the permanent wave, and while I skeen them, and make them the dimples and the sweet smiles. They suffer so, the poor dears, and eef you would seet and hold their hands, they would love eet, they would come every day for eet, and you would be famous, and you would be reech. You would meet—oh, such lovely ladies! The best people in the ceety come to my beauty parlors, and they would adore you, Meester Carpentair—what do you say to eet?"

It struck me as curious, as I looked back upon it; Madame Planchet so far had not heard the sound of Carpenter's voice. Now she forced him to speak, but she did not force him to look at her. His gaze went over her head, as if he were seeing a vision; he recited:

"Because the daughters of Zion are haughty, and walk with stretched forth necks and wanton eyes, walking and mincing as they go, and making a tinkling with their feet; therefore the Lord will smite with a scab the crown of the head of the daughters of Zion, and the Lord will discover their secret parts."

"Oh, mon Dieu!" cried Madame Planchet.

"In that day the Lord will take away the bravery of their twinkling ornaments about their feet, and their cauls, and their round tires like the moon, the chains, and the bracelets, and the mufflers, the bonnets, and the ornaments of the legs, and the headbands, and the tablets, and the earrings, the rings and nose jewels, the changeable suits of apparel, and the mantles, and the wimples, and the crisping pins, the glasses, and the fine linen, and the hoods, and the veils. And it shall come to pass that instead of sweet smell there shall be stink; and instead of a girdle a rent; and instead of well set hair, baldness; and instead of a stomacher a girding of sackcloth: and burning instead of beauty."

And at that moment the door from the corridor was flung open, and Mary Magna came in.

XI

"My God, will you look who's here! Billy, wretched creature, I haven't laid eyes on you for two months! Do you have to desert me entirely, just because you've fallen in love with a society girl with the face of a Japanese doll-baby? What's the matter with me, that I lose my lovers faster than I get them? Edgerton Rosythe, come in here—you've got a good excuse, I admit—I'm almost as much scared of your wife as you are yourself. But still, I'd like a chance to get tired of some man first. Hello, Planchet, how's my old grannie making out in your scalping-shop? Say, would you think it would take three days labor for half a dozen Sioux squaws to pull the skin off one old lady's back? And a week to tie up the corners of her mouth and give her a permanent smile! 'Why, grannie,' I said, 'good God, it would be cheaper to hire Charlie Chaplin to walk round in front of you all the rest of your life!' And—why, what's this? For the love of Peter, somebody introduce me to this gentleman. Is he a friend of yours, Billy? Carpenter? Excuse me, Mr. Carpenter, but we picture people learn to talk about our faces and our styles, and it isn't every day I come on a million dollars walking round on two legs. Who does the gentleman work for?"

The storm of Mary Magna stopped long enough for her to stare from one to another of us. "What? You mean nobody's got him? And you all standing round here, not signing any contracts? You, Edgerton—you haven't run to the telephone to call up Eternal City? Well, as it happens, T-S is going to be here in five minutes—his wife is being made beautiful once again somewhere in this scalping-shop. Take my advice, Mr. Carpenter, and don't sign today—the price will go up several hundred per week as long as you hold off."

Mary stopped again; and this was most unusual, for as a general rule she never stopped until somebody or something stopped her. But she was fascinated by the spectacle of Carpenter. "My good God! Where did he come from? Why, it seems like—I'm trying to think—yes, it's the very man! Listen, Billy; you may not believe it, but I was in a church a couple of weeks ago. I went to see Roxanna Riddle marry that grand duke fellow. It was in a big church over by the park—St. Bartholomew's, they call it. I sat looking at a stained glass window over the altar, and Billy, I swear I believe this Mr. Carpenter came down from that window!"

"Maybe he did, Mary," I put in.

"But I'm not joking! I tell you he's the living, speaking image of that figure. Come to think of it, he isn't speaking, he hasn't said a word! Tell me, Mr. Carpenter, have you got a voice, or are you only a close up from 'The Servant in the House' or 'Ben Hur'? Say something, so I can get a line on you!"

Again I stood wondering; how would Carpenter take this? Would he bow his head and run before a hail-storm of feminine impertinence? Would she "vamp" him, as she did every man who came near her? Or would this man do what no man alive had yet been able to do—reduce her to silence?

He smiled gently; and I saw that she had vamped him this much, at least—he was going to be polite! "Mary," he said, "I think you are carrying everything but the nose jewels."

"Nose jewels? What a horrid idea! Where did you get that?"

"When you came in, I was quoting the prophet Isaiah. Some eighty generations of ladies have lived on earth since his day, Mary; they have won the ballot, but apparently they haven't discovered anything new in the way of ornaments. Some of the prophet's words may be strange to you, but if you study them you will see that you've got everything he lists: 'their tinkling ornaments about their feet, and their cauls, and their round tires like the moon, the chains, and the bracelets, and the mufflers, the bonnets, and the ornaments of the legs, and the headbands, and the tablets, and the earrings, the rings, and nose jewels, the changeable suits of apparel, and the mantles, and the wimples, and the crisping pins, the glasses, and the fine linen, and the hoods, and the veils.'"

As Carpenter recited this list, his eyes roamed from one part to another of the wondrous "get up" of Mary Magna. You can imagine her facing him—that bold and vivid figure which you have seen as "Cleopatra" and "Salome," as "Dubarry" and "Anne Boleyn," and I know not how many other of the famous courtesans and queens of history. In daily life her style and manner is every bit as staggering; she is a gorgeous brunette, and wears all the colors there are—when she goes down the street it is like a whole procession with flags. I'll wager that, apart from her jewels, which may or may not have been real, she was carrying not less than five thousand dollars worth of stuff that fall afternoon. A big black picture hat, with a flower garden and parts of an aviary on top—but what's the use of going over Isaiah's list?

"Everything but the nose jewels," said Carpenter, "and they may be in fashion next week."

"How about the glasses?" put in Rosythe, entering into the fun.

"Oh, shucks!" said I, protecting my friend. "Turn out the contents of your vanity-bag, Mary."

"And the crisping-pins?" laughed the critic.

"Hasn't Madame Planchet just shown us those?"

All this while Mary had not taken her eyes off Carpenter. "So you are really one of those religious fellows!" she exclaimed. "You'll know exactly what to do without any directing! How perfectly incredible!" And at that appropriate moment T-S pushed open the door and waddled in!

XII

YOU know the screen stars, of course; but maybe you do not know those larger celestial bodies, the dark and silent and invisible stars from which the shining ones derive their energies. So, permit me to introduce you to T-S, the trade abbreviation for a name which nobody can remember, which even his secretaries have to keep typed on a slip of paper just above their machine—Tszchniczklefritszch. He came a few years ago from Ruthenia, or Rumelia, or Roumania—one of those countries where the consonants are so greatly in excess of the vowels. If you are as rich as he, you call him Abey, which is easy; otherwise, you call him Mr. T-S, which he accepts as a part of his Americanization.

He is shorter than you or I, and has found that he can't grow upward, but can grow without limit in all lateral directions. There is always a little more of him than his clothing can hold, and it spreads out in rolls about his collar. He has a yellowish face, which turns red easily. He has small, shiny eyes, he speaks atrocious English, he is as devoid of culture as a hairy Ainu, and he smells money and goes after it like a hog into a swill-trough.

"Hello, everybody! Madame, vere's de old voman?

"She ees being dressed—"

"Vell, speed her up! I got no time. I got—Jesus Christ!"

"Yes, exactly," said Mary Magna.

The great man of the pictures stood rooted to the spot. "Vot's dis? Some joke you people playin' on me?" He shot a suspicious glance from one to another of us.

"No," said Mary, "he's real. Honest to God!"

"Oh! You bring him for an engagement. Vell, I don't do no business outside my office. Send him to see Lipsky in de mornin'."

"He hasn't asked for an engagement," said Mary.

"Oh, he ain't. Vell, vot's he hangin' about for? Been gittin' a permanent vave? Ha, ha, ha!"

"Cut it out, Abey," said Mary Magna. "This is a gentleman, and you must be decent. Mr. Carpenter, meet Mr. T-S."

"Carpenter, eh? Vell, Mr. Carpenter, if I vas to make a picture vit you I gotta spend a million dollars on it—you know you can't make no cheap skate picture fer a ting like dat, if you do you got a piece o' cheese. It'd gotta be a costume picture, and you got shoost as much show to market vun o' dem today as you got vit a pauper's funeral. I spend all dat money, and no show to git it back, and den you actors tink I'm makin' ten million a veek off you—"

"Cut it out, Abey!" broke in Mary. "Mr. Carpenter hasn't asked anything of you."

"Oh, he ain't, hey? So dat's his game. Vell, he'll find maybe I can vait as long as de next feller. Ven he gits ready to talk business, he knows vere Eternal City is, I guess. Vot's de matter, Madame, you got dat old voman o' mine melted to de chair?"

"I'll see, I'll see, Meester T-S," said Madame, hustling out of the room.

Mary came up to the great man. "See here, Abey," she said, in a low voice, "you're making the worst mistake of your life. Apparently this man hasn't been discovered. When he is, you know what'll happen."

"Vere doss he come from?"

"I don't know. Billy here brought him. I said he must have come out of a stained glass window in St. Bartholomew's Church."

"Oho, ho!" said T-S.

"Anyhow, he's new, and he's too good to keep. The paper's 'll get hold of him sure. Just look at him!"

"But, Mary, can he act?"

"Act? My God, he don't have to act! He only has to look at you, and you want to fall at his feet. Go be decent to him, and find out what he wants."

The great man surveyed the figure of the stranger appraisingly. Then he went up to him. "See here, Mr. Carpenter, maybe I could make you famous. Vould you like dat?"

"I have never thought of being famous," was the reply.

"Vell, you tink of it now. If I hire you, I make you de greatest actor in de vorld. I make it a propaganda picture fer de churches, dey vould show it to de headens in China and in Zululand. I make you a contract fer ten years, and I pay you five hunded dollars a veek, vedder you vork or not, and you vouldn't have to vork so much, because I don't catch myself makin' a million dollar feature picture vit gawd amighty and de angels in it for no regular veekly releases. Maybe you find some cheap skate feller vit some vild cat company vot promise you more; but he sells de picture and makes over de money to his vife's brudders, and den he goes bust, and vere you at den, hey? Mary Magna, here, she tell you, if you git a contract vit old Abey, it's shoost like you got libbidy bonds. I make dat lovely lady a check every veek fer tirty-five hunded dollars, an' I gotta sign it vit my own hand, and I tell you it gives me de cramps to sign so much money all de time, but I do it, and you see all dem rings and ribbons and veils and tings vot she buys vit de money, she looks like a jeweler's shop and a toy-store all rolled into vun goin' valkin' down de street."

"Mr. Carpenter was just scolding me for that," said Mary. "I've an idea if you pay him a salary, he'll feed it to the poor."

"If I pay it," said T-S, "it's his, and he can feed it to de dicky-birds if he vants to. Vot you say, Mr. Carpenter?"

I was waiting with curiosity to hear what he would say; but at that moment the door from the "maternity-room" was opened, and the voice of Madame Planchet broke in: "Here she ees!" And the flesh-mountain appeared, with the two caryatids supporting her.

XIII

"My Gawd!" gasped Mrs. T-S. "I'm dyin'!"

Her husband responded, beaming, "So you gone and done it again!"

Said Mrs. T-S: "I'll never do it no more!"

Said the husband: "Y'allus say dat. Fergit it, Maw, you're all right now, you don't have to have your hair frizzed fer six mont's!"

Said Mrs. T-S: "I gotta lie down. I'm dyin', Abey, I tell you. Lemme git on de sofa."

Said the husband: "Now, Maw, we gotta git to dinner—"

"I can't eat no dinner."

"Vot?" There was genuine alarm in the husband's voice. "You can't eat no dinner? Sure you gotta eat your dinner. You can't live if you don't eat. Come along now, Maw."

"O-o-o-o-o-o-o-o-oh!"

T-S went and stood before her, and a grin came over his face. "Sure, now, ain't it fine? Say, Mary, look at dem lovely curves. Billy, shoost look here! Vy, she looks like a kid again, don't she! Madame, you're a daisy—you sure deliver de goods."

Madame Planchet beamed, and the flesh-mountain was feebly cheered. "You like it, Abey?"

"Sure, I like it! Maw, it's grand! It's like I got a new girl! Come on now, git up, we go git our dinner, and den we gotta see dem night scenes took. Don't forgit, we're payin' two tousand men five dollars apiece tonight, and we gotta git our money out of 'em." Then, taking for granted that this settled it, he turned to the rest. "You come vit us, Mary?"

"I must wait for my grannie."

"Sure, you leave your car fer grannie, and you come vit us, and we git some dinner, and den we see dem mob scenes took. You come along, Mr. Carpenter, I gotta have some talk vit you. And you, Billy? And Rosythe—come, pile in."

"I have to wait for the missus," said the critic. "We have a date."

"Vell, said T-S, and he went up close. "You do me a favor, Rosythe; don't say nuttin' about dis fellow Carpenter tonight. I feed him and git him feelin' good, and den I make a contract vit him, and I give you a front page telegraph story, see?"

"All right," said the critic.

"Mum's de vord now," said the magnate; and he waddled out, and the two caryatids lifted the flesh-mountain, and half carried it to the elevator, and Mary walked with Carpenter, and I brought up the rear.

The car of T-S was waiting at the door, and this car is something special. It is long, like a freight-car, made all of shining gun-metal, or some such material; the huge wheels are of solid metal, and the fenders are so big and solid, it looks like an armored military car. There is an extra wheel on each side, and two more locked on to the rear. There is a chauffeur in uniform, and a footman in uniform, just to open the doors and close them and salute you as you enter.

Inside, it is all like the sofas in Madame's scalping shop; you fall into them, and soft furs enfold you, and you give a sigh of Contentment, "O-o-o-o-o-o-oh!"

"Prince's," said T-S to the chauffeur, and the palace on wheels began to glide along. It occurred to me to wonder that T-S was not embarrassed to take Carpenter to a fashionable eating-place. But I could read his thoughts; everybody would assume that he had been "on location" with one of his stars; and anyhow, what the hell? Wasn't he Abey Tszchniczklefritszch?

"Wor-r-r-r-r! Wor-r-r-r-r-r!" snarled the horn of the car; and I could understand the meaning of this also. It said: "I am the car of Abey Tszchniczklefritszch, king of the movies, future king of the world. Get the hell out o' my way!" So we sped through the crowded streets, and pedestrians scattered like autumn leaves before a storm. "My Gawd, but I'm hungry!" said T-S. "I ain't had nuttin' to eat since lunch-time. How goes it, Maw? Feelin' better? Vell, you be all right ven you git your grub."

So we came to Prince's, and drew up before the porte-cochere, and found ourselves confronting an adventure. There was a crowd before the place, a surging throng half-way down the block, with a whole line of policemen to hold them back. Over the heads of the crowd were transparencies, frame boxes with canvas on, and lights inside, and words painted on them. "Hello!" cried T-S. "Vot's dis?"

Suddenly I recalled what I had read in the morning's paper. The workers of the famous lobster palace had gone on strike, and trouble was feared. I told T-S, and he exclaimed: "Oh, hell! Ain't we got troubles enough vit strikers in de studios, vitout dey come spoilin' our dinner?"

The footman had jumped from his seat, and had the door open, and the great man began to alight. At that moment the mob set up a howl. "For shame! For shame! Unfair! Don't go in there! They starve their workers! They're taking the bread out of our mouths! Scabs! Scabs!"

I got out second, and saw a spectacle of haggard faces, shouting menaces and pleadings; I saw hands waved wildly, one or two fists clenched; I saw the police, shoving against the mass, poking with their sticks, none too gently. A poor devil in a waiter's costume stretched out his arms to me, yelling in a foreign dialect: "You take de food from my babies!" The next moment the club of a policeman came down on his head, crack. I heard Mary scream behind me, and I turned, just in the nick of time. Carpenter was leaping toward the policeman, crying, "Stop!"

There was no chance to parley in this emergency. I grabbed Carpenter in a foot-ball tackle. I got one arm pinned to his side, and Mary, good old scout, got the other as quickly. She is a bit of an athlete—has to keep in training for those hoochie-coochies and things she does, when she wins the love of emperors and sultans and such-like world-conquerors. Also, when we got hold of Carpenter, we discovered that he wasn't much but skin and bones anyhow. We fairly lifted him up and rushed him into the restaurant; and after the first moment he stopped resisting, and let us lead him between the aisles of diners, on the heels of the toddling T-S. There was a table reserved, in an alcove, and we brought him to it, and then waited to see what we had done.

XIV

CARPENTER turned to me-and those sad but everchangjng eyes were flashing. "You have taken a great liberty!"

"There wasn't any time to argue," I said. "If you knew what I know about the police of Western City and their manners, you wouldn't want to monkey with them."

Mary backed me up earnestly. "They'd have mashed your face, Mr. Carpenter."

"My face?" he repeated. "Is not a man more than his face?"

You should have heard the shout of T-S! "Vot? Ain't I shoost offered you five hunded dollars a veek fer dat face, and you vant to go git it smashed? And fer a lot o' lousy bums dat vont vork for honest vages, and vont let nobody else vork! Honest to Gawd, Mr. Carpenter, I tell you some stories about strikes vot we had on our own lot—you vouldn't spoil your face for such lousy sons-o'-guns—"

"Ssh, Abey, don't use such langwich, you should to be shamed of yourself!" It was Maw, guardian of the proprieties, who had been extracted from the car by the footman, and helped to the table.

"Vell, Mr. Carpenter, he dunno vot dem fellers is like—"

"Sit down, Abey!" commanded the old lady. "Ve ain't ordered no stump speeches fer our dinner."

We seated ourselves. And Carpenter turned his dark eyes on me. "I observe that you have many kinds of mobs in your city," he remarked. "And the police do interfere with some of them."

"My Gawd!" cried T-S. "You gonna have a lot o' bums jumpin' on people ven dey try to git to dinner?"

Said Carpenter: "Mr. Rosythe said that the police would not work unless they were paid. May I ask, who pays them to work here? Is it the proprietor of the restaurant?"

"Vell," cried T-S, "ain't he gotta take care of his place?"

"As a matter of fact," said I, laughing, "from what I read in the 'Times' this morning, I gather that an old friend of Mr. Carpenter's has been paying in this case."

Carpenter looked at me inquiringly.

"Mr. Algernon de Wiggs, president of the Chamber of Commerce, issued a statement denouncing the way the police were letting mobs of strikers interfere with business, and proposing that the Chamber take steps to stop it. You remember de Wiggs, and how we left him?"

"Yes, I remember," said Carpenter; and we exchanged a smile over that trick we had played.

I could see T-S prick forward his ears. "Vot? You know de Viggs?"

"Mr. Carpenter possesses an acquaintance with our best society which will astonish you when you realize it."

"Vy didn't you tell me dat?" demanded the other; and I could complete the sentence for him: "Somebody has offered him more money!"

Here the voice of Maw was heard: "Ain't we gonna git nuttin' to eat?"

So for a time the problem of capital and labor was put to one side. There were two waiters standing by, very nervous, because of the strike. T-S grabbed the card from one, and read off a list of food, which the waiter wrote down. Maw, who was learning the rudiments of etiquette, handed her card to Mary, who gave her order, and then Maw gave hers, and I gave mine, and there was only Carpenter left.

He was sitting, his dark eyes roaming here and there about the dining-room. Prince's, as you may know, is a gorgeous establishment: too much so for my taste—it has almost as much gilded moulding as if T-S had designed it for a picture palace. In front of Carpenter's eyes sat a dame with a bare white back, and a rope of big pearls about it, and a tiara of diamonds on top; and beyond her were more dames, and yet more, and men in dinner-coats, putting food into red faces. You and I get used to such things, but I could understand that to a stranger it must be shocking to see so many people feeding so expensively.

"Vot you vant to order, Mr. Carpenter?" demanded T-S; and I waited, full of curiosity. What would this man choose to eat in a "lobster palace"?

Carpenter took the card from his host and studied it. Apparently he had no difficulty in finding the most substantial part of the menu. "I'll have prime ribs of beef," said he; "and boiled mutton with caper sauce; and young spring turkey; and squab en casserole; and milk fed guinea fowl—" The waiter, of course, was obediently writing down each item. "And planked steak with mushrooms; and braised spare ribs—"

"My Gawd!" broke in the host.

"And roast teal duck; and lamb kidneys—"

"Fer the love o' Mike, Mr. Carpenter, you gonna eat all dat?"

"No; of course not."

"Den vot you gonna do vit it?"

"I'm going to take it to the hungry men outside."

Well, sir, you'd have thought the world had stopped turning round, so still it was. The two waiters nearly dropped their order-pads and their napkins; they did drop their jaws, and Mrs. T-S's permanent wave seemed about to go flat.

"Oh, hell!" cried T-S at last. You can't do it!"

"I can't?"

"You can't order only vot you gonna eat."

"But then, I don't want anything. I'm not hungry."

"But you can't sit here like a dummy, man!" He turned to the waiter. "You bring him de same vot you bring me. Unnerstand? And git a move on, cause I'm starvin'. Fade out now!" And the waiter turned and fled.

XV

THE proprietor of Eternal City wiped his perspiring forehead with his napkin, and started rather hurriedly to make conversation. I understood that he wanted to enjoy his dinner, and proposed to talk about something pleasant in the meantime. "I vonna tell you about dis picture ve're goin' to see took, Mr. Carpenter. I vant you should see de scale we do tings on, ven we got a big subjic. Y'unnerstand, dis is a feature picture ve're makin' now; a night picture, a big mob scene.".

"Mob scene?" said Carpenter. "You have so many mobs in this world of yours!"

"Vell, sure," said T-S. "You gotta take dis vorld de vay you find it. Y'can't change human nature, y'know. But dis vot you're gonna see tonight is only a play mob, y'unnerstand."

"That is what seems strangest of all to me," said the other, thoughtfully. "You like mobs so well that you make imitation ones!"

"Vell, de people, dey like to see crowds in a picture, and dey like to see action. If you gonna have a big picture, you gotta spend de money."

"Why not take this real mob that is outside the door?"

"Ha, ha, ha! Ve couldn't verk dat very good, Mr. Carpenter. Ve gotta have it in de right set; and ven you git a real mob, it don't alvays do vot you vant exactly! Besides, you can't take night pictures unless you got your lights and everyting. No, ve gotta make our mobs to order; we got two tousand fellers hired—"

"What Mr. Rosythe called 'studio bums'? You have that many?"

"Sure, we could git ten tousand if de set vould hold 'em. Dis picture is called 'De Tale o' Two Cities,' and it's de French revolution. It's about a feller vot takes anodder feller's place and gits his head cut off; and say, dere's a sob story in it vot's a vunder. Ven dey brought me de scenario, I says, 'Who's de author?' Dey says, 'It's a guy named Charles Dickens.' 'Dickens?' says I. 'Vell, I like his verk. Vot's his address?' And Lipsky, he says, says he, 'Dey tell me he stays in a place called Vestminster Abbey, in England.' 'Vell,' says I, 'send him a cablegram and find out vot he'll take fer an exclusive contract.' So we sent a cablegram to Charles Dickens, Vestminster Abbey, England, and we didn't git no answer, and come to find out, de boys in de studios vas havin' a laugh on old Abey, because dis guy Dickens is some old time feller, and de Abbey is vere dey got his bones. Vell, dey can have deir fun—how de hell's a feller like me gonna git time to know about writers? Vy, only twelve years ago, Maw here and me vas carryin' pants in a push-cart fer a livin', and we didn't know if a book vas top-side up or bottom—ain't it, Maw?"

Maw certified that it was—though I thought not quite so eagerly as her husband. There were five little T-S's growing up, and bringing pressure to let the dead past stay buried, in Vestminster Abbey or wherever it might be.

The waiter brought the dinner, and spread it before us. And T-S tucked his napkin under both ears, and grabbed his knife in one hand and his fork in the other, and took a long breath, and said: "Good-bye, folks. See you later!" And he went to work.

XVI

FOR five minutes or so there was no sound but that of one man's food going in and going down. Then suddenly the man stopped, with his knife and fork upright on the table in each hand, and cried: "Mr. Carpenter, you ain't eatin' nuttin'!"

The stranger, who had apparently been in a daydream, came suddenly back to Prince's. He looked at the quantities of food spread about him. "If you'd only let me take a little to those men outside!" He said it pleadingly.

But T-S tapped imperiously on the table, with both his knife and fork together. "Mr. Carpenter, eat your dinner! Eat it, now, I say!" It was as if he were dealing with one of the five little T-S's. And Carpenter, strange as it may seem, obeyed. He picked up a bit of bread, and began to nibble it, and T-S went to work again.

There was another five minutes of silence; and then the picture magnate stopped, with a look of horror on his face. "My Gawd! He's cryin'!" Sure enough, there were two large tears trickling, one down each cheek of the stranger, and dropping on the bread he was putting into his mouth!

"Look here, Mr. Carpenter," protested T-S. "Is it dem strikers?"

"I'm sorry; you see—"

"Now, honest, man, vy should you spoil your dinner fer a bunch o' damn lousy loafers—"

"Abey, vot a vay to talk at a dinner-party!" broke in Maw.

And then suddenly Mary Magna spoke. It was a strange thing, though I did not realize it until afterwards. Mary, the irrepressible, had hardly said one word since we left the beauty parlors! Mary, always the life of dinner parties, was sitting like a woman who had seen the ghost of a dead child; her eyes following Carpenter's, her mind evidently absorbed in probing his thoughts.

"Abey!" said she, with sudden passion, of a sort I'd never seen her display before. "Forget your grub for a moment, I have something to say. Here's a man with a heart full of love for other people—while you and I are just trying to see what we can get out of them! A man who really has a religion—and you're trying to turn him into a movie doll! Try to get it through your skull, Abey!"

The great man's eyes were wide open. "Holy smoke, Mary! Vot's got into you?" And suddenly he almost shrieked. "Lord! She's cryin' too!"

"No, I'm not," declared Mary, vialiantly. But there were two drops on her cheeks, so big that she was forced to wipe them away. "It's just a little shame, that's all. Here we sit, with three times as much food before us as we can eat; and all over this city are poor devils with nothing to eat, and no homes to go to—don't you know that's true, Abey? Don't you know it, Maw?"

"Looka here, kid," said the magnate; "you know vot'll happen to you if you git to broodin' over tings? You git your face full o' wrinkles—you already gone and spoilt your make-up."

"Shucks, Abey," broke in Maw, "vot you gotta do vit dat? Vy don't you mind your own business?"

"Mind my own business? My own business, you say? Vell, I like to know vot you call my business! Ven I got a contract to pay a girl tirty-five hunded dollars a veek fer her face, and she goes and gits it all wrinkles, I ask any jury, is it my business or ain't it? And if a feller vants to pull de tremulo stop fer a lot o' hoboes and Bullsheviki, and goes and spills his tears into his soup—"

It sounded fierce; but Mary apparently knew her Abey; also, she saw that Maw was starting to cry. "There's no use trying to bluff me, Abey. You know as well as I do there are hungry people in this city, and no fault of theirs. You know, too, you eat twice what you ought to, because I've heard the doctor tell you. I'm not blaming you a bit more than I do myself—me, with two automobiles, and a whole show-window on my back." And suddenly she turned to Carpenter. "What can we do?"

He answered: "Here, men gorge themselves; in Russia they are eating their dead."

T-S dropped his knife and fork, and Maw gave a gulp. "Oh, my Gawd!"

"There are ten million people doomed to starve. Their children eat grass, and their bellies swell up and their legs dwindle to broom-sticks; they stagger and fall into the ditches, and other children tear their flesh and devour it."

"O-o-o-o-o-o-o-o-oh!" wailed Maw; and the diners at Prince's began to stare.

"Now looka here!" cried T-S, wildly. "I say dis ain't no decent way to behave at a party. I say it ain't on de level to be a feller's guest, and den jump on him and spoil his dinner. See here, Mr. Carpenter, I tell you vot I do. You be good and eat your grub, so it don't git vasted, and I promise you, tomorrow I go and hunt up strike headquarters, and give dem a check fer a tousand dollars, and if de damn graftin' leaders don't hog it, dey all git someting to eat. And vot's more, I send a check fer five tousand to de Russian relief. Now ain't dat square? Vot you say?"

"What I say is, Mr. T-S, I cannot be the keeper of another man's conscience. But I'll try to eat, so as not to be rude."

And T-S grunted, and went back to his feeding; and the stranger made a pretense of eating, and we did the same.

XVII

IT happens that I was brought up in a highly conscientious family. To my dear mother, and to her worthy sisters, there is nothing in the world more painful than what they call a "scene"—unless possibly it is what they call a "situation." And here we had certainly had a "scene," and still had a "situation." So I sat, racking my brains to think of something safe to talk about. I recalled that T-S had had pretty good success with his "Tale of Two Cities" as a topic of Conversation, so I began:

"Mr. Carpenter, the spectacle you are going to see this evening is rather remarkable from the artistic point of view. One of the greatest scenic artists of Paris has designed the set, and the best judges consider it a real achievement, a landmark in moving picture work."

"Tell me about it," said Carpenter; and I was grateful for his tone of interest.

"Well, I don't know how much you know about picture making—"

"You had better explain everything."

"Well, Mr. T-S has built a large set, representing a street scene in Paris over a century ago. He has hired a thousand men—"

"Two tousand!" broke in T-S.

"In the advertisements?" I suggested, with a smile.

"No, no," insisted the other. "Two tousand, really. In de advertisements, five tousand."

"Well," said I, "these men wear costumes which T-S has had made for them, and they pretend to be a mob. They have been practicing all day, and by now they know what to do. There is a man with a megaphone, shouting orders to them, and enormous lights playing upon them, so that men with cameras can take pictures of the scene. It is very vivid, and as a portrayal of history, is truly educational."

"And when it is done—what becomes of the men?"

Utterly hopeless, you see! We were right back on the forbidden ground! "How do you mean?" I evaded.

"I mean, how do they live?"

"Dey got deir five dollars, ain't dey?" It was T-S, of course.

"Yes, but that won' last very long, will it? What is the cost of this dinner we are eating?"

The magnate of the movies looked to the speaker, and then burst into a laugh. "Ho, ho, ho! Dat's a good vun!"

Said I, hastily: "Mr. T-S means that there are cheaper eating places to be found."

"Well," said Carpenter, "why don't we find one?"

"It's no use, Billy. He thinks it's up to me to feed all de bums on de lot. Is dat it, Mr. Carpenter?"

"I can't say, Mr. T-S; I don't know how many there are, and I don't know how rich you are."

"Vell, dey got five million out o' verks in this country now, and if I vanted to bust myself, I could feed 'em vun day, maybe two. But ven I got done, dey vouldn't be nobody to make pictures, and somebody vould have to feed old Abey—or maybe me and Maw could go back to carryin' pants in a push cart! If you tink I vouldn't like to see all de hungry fed, you got me wrong, Mr. Carpenter; but vot I learned is dis—if you stop fer all de misery you see in de vorld about you, you vouldn't git novhere."

"Well," said Carpenter, "what difference would that make?"

The proprietor of Eternal City really wanted to make out the processes of this abnormal mind. He wrinkled his brows, and thought very hard over it.

"See here, Mr. Carpenter," he began at last, "I tink you got hold o' de wrong feller. I'm a verkin' man, de same as any mechanic on my lot. I verked ever since I vas a liddle boy, and if I eat too much now, maybe it's because I didn't get enough ven I vas liddle. And maybe I got more money dan vot I got a right to, but I know dis—I ain't never had enough to do half vot I vant to! But dere's plenty fellers got ten times vot I got, and never done a stroke o' vork fer it. Dey're de vuns y'oughter git after!"

Said Carpenter: "I would, if I knew how."

"Dey's plenty of 'em right in dis room, I bet." And Mary added: "Ask Billy; he knows them all!"

"You flatter me, Mary," I laughed.

"Ain't dey some of 'em here?" demanded T-S.

"Yes, that's true. There are some not far away, who are developing a desire to meet Mr. Carpenter, unless I miss the signs."

"Vere are dey at?" demanded T-S.

"I won't tell you that," I laughed, "because you'd turn and stare into their faces."

"So he vould!" broke in Maw. "How often I gotta tell you, Abey? You got no more manners dan if you vas a jimpanzy."

"All right," said the magnate, grinning good naturedly. "I'll keep a-eatin' my dinner. Who is it?"

"It's Mrs. Parmelee Stebbins," said I. "She boasts a salon, and has to have what are called lions, and she's been watching Mr. Carpenter out of the corner of her eye ever since he came into the room—trying to figure out whether he's a lion, or only an actor. If his skin were a bit dark, she would be sure he was an Eastern potentate; as it, she's afraid he's of domestic origin, in which case he's vulgar. The company he keeps is against him; but still—Mrs. Stebbins has had my eye three times, hoping I would give her a signal, I haven't given it, so she's about to leave."

"Vell, she can go to hell!" said T-S, keeping his promise to devote himself to his dinner. "I offered Parmelee Stebbins a tird share in 'De Pride o' Passion' fer a hunded tousand dollars, and de damn fool turned me down, and de picture has made a million and a quarter a'ready."

"Well," said I, "he's probably paying for it by sitting up late to buy the city council on this new franchise grab of his; and so he hasn't kept his date to dine with his expensive family at Prince's. Here is Miss Lucinda Stebbins; she's engaged to Babcock, millionaire sport and man about town, but he's taking part in a flying race over the Rocky Mountains tonight, and so Lucinda feels bored, and she knows the vaudeville show is going to be tiresome, but still she doesn't want to meet any freaks. She has just said to her mother that she can't see why a person in her mother's position can't be content to meet proper people, but always has to be getting herself into the newspapers with some new sort of nut."

"My Gawd, Billy!" cried Maw. "You got a dictaphone on dem people?"

"No, but I know the type so well, I can tell by their looks. Lucinda is thinking about their big new palace on Grand Avenue, and she regards everyone outside her set as a burglar trying to break in. And then there's Bertie Stebbins, who's thinking about a new style of collar he saw advertised to-day, and how it would look on him, and what impression it would make on his newest girl."

It was Mary who spoke now: "I know that little toad. I've seen him dancing at the Palace with Dorothy Doodles, or whatever her name is."

"Well," said I, "Mrs. Stebbins runs the newer set—those who hunt sensations, and make a splurge in the papers. It costs like smoke, of course—" And suddenly I stopped. "Look out!" I whispered. "Here she comes!"

XVIII

I heard Maw catch her breath, and I heard Maw's husband give a grunt. Then I rose. "How are you, Billy?" gurgled a voice—one of those voices made especially for social occasions. "Wretched boy, why do you never come to see us?"

"I was coming to-morrow," I said—for who could prove otherwise? "Mrs. Stebbins, permit me to introduce Mrs. Tszchniczklefritszch."

"Charmed to meet you, I'm sure," said Mrs. Stebbins. "I've heard my husband speak of your husband so often. How well you are looking, Mrs.—"

She stopped; and Maw, knowing the terrors of her name, made haste to say something agreeable. "Yes, ma'am; dis country agrees vit me fine. Since I come here, I've rode and et, shoost rode and et."

"And Mr. T-S," said I.

"Howdydo, Mr. T-S?"

"Pretty good, ma'am," said T-S. He had been caught with his mouth full, and was making desperate efforts to swallow.

A singular thing is the power of class prestige! Here was Maw, a good woman, according to her lights, who had worked hard all her life, and had achieved a colossal and astounding success. She had everything in the world that money could buy; her hair was done by the best hair-dresser, her gown had been designed by the best costumer, her rings and bracelets selected by the best jeweller; and yet nothing was right, no power on earth could make it right, and Maw knew it, and writhed the consciousness of it. And here was Mrs. Parmelee Stebbins, who had never done a useful thing in all her days—except you count the picking out of a rich husband; yet Mrs. Stebbins was "right," and Maw knew it, and in the presence of the other woman she was in an utter panic, literally quivering in every nerve. And here was old T-S, who, left to himself, might have really meant what he said, that Mrs. Stebbins could go to hell; but because he was married, and loved his wife, he too trembled, and gulped down his food!

Mrs. Stebbins is one of those American matrons who do not allow marriage and motherhood to make vulgar physical impressions upon them. Her pale blue gown might have been worn by her daughter; her cool grey eyes looked out through a face without a wrinkle from a soul without a care. She was a patroness of art and intellect; but never did she forget her fundamental duty, the enhancing of the prestige of a family name. When she was introduced to a screen-actress, she was gracious, but did not forget the difference between an actress and a lady. When she was introduced to a strange man who did not wear trousers, she took it quite as an everyday matter, revealing no trace of vulgar human curiosity.

There came Bertie, full grown, but not yet out of the pimply stage, and still conscious of the clothes which he had taken such pains to get right. Bertie's sister remained in her seat, refusing naughtily to be compromised by her mother's vagaries; but Bertie had a purpose, and after I had introduced him round, I saw what he wanted—Mary Magna! Bertie had a vision of himself as a sort of sporting prince in this movie world. His social position would make conquests easy; it was a sort of Christmas-tree, all a-glitter with prizes.

I was standing near, and heard the beginning of their conversation. "Oh, Miss Magna, I'm so pleased to meet you. I've heard so much about you from Miss Dulles."

"Miss Dulles?"

"Yes; Dorothy Dulles."

"I'm sorry. I don't think I ever heard of her."

"What? Dorothy Dulles, the screen actress?"

"No, I can't place her."

"But—but she's a star!"

"Well, but you know, Mr. Stebbins—there are so many stars in the heavens, and not all of them visible to the eye."

I turned to Bertie's mamma. She had discovered that Carpenter looked even more thrilling on a close view; he was not a stage figure, but a really grave and impressive personality, exactly the thing to thrill the ladies of the Higher Arts Club at their monthly luncheon, and to reflect prestige upon his discoverer. So here she was, inviting the party to share her box at the theatre; and here was T-S explaining that it couldn't be done, he had got to see his French revolution pictures took, dey had five tousand men hired to make a mob. I noted that Mrs. Stebbins received the "advertising" figures on the production!

The upshot of it was that the great lady consented to forget her box at the theatre, and run out to the studios to see the mob scenes for the "The Tale of Two Cities." T-S hadn't quite finished his dinner, but he waved his hand and said it was nuttin', he vouldn't keep Mrs. Stebbins vaitin'. He beckoned the waiter, and signed his magic name on the check, with a five-dollar bill on top for a tip. Mrs. Stebbins collected her family and floated to the door, and our party followed.

I expected another scene with the mob; but I found that the street had been swept clear of everything but policemen and chauffeurs. I knew that this must have meant rough work on the part of the authorities, but I said nothing, and hoped that Carpenter would not think of it. The Stebbins car drew up by the porte-cochere; and suddenly I discovered why the wife of the street-car magnate was known as a "social leader." "Billy," she said, "you come in our car, and bring Mr. Carpenter; I have something to talk to you about." Just that easily, you see! She wanted something, so she asked for it!

I took Carpenter by the arm and put him in. Bertie drove, the chauffeur sitting in the seat beside him. "Beat you to it!" called Bertie, with his invincible arrogance, and waved his hand to the picture magnate as we rolled away.

XIX

AS it happened, we made a poor start. Turning the corner into Broadway, we found ourselves caught in the jam of the theatre traffic, and our car was brought to a halt in front of the "Empire Varieties." If you have been on any Broadway between the Atlantic and Pacific oceans, you can imagine the sight; the flaring electric signs, the pictures of the head line artists, the people waiting to buy tickets, and the crowds on the sidewalk pushing past. There was one additional feature, a crowd of "rah-rah boys," with yellow and purple flags in their hands, and the glory of battle in their eyes. As our car halted, the cheer-leader gave a signal, and a hundred throats let out in unison:

> "Rickety zim, rickety zam,
> Brickety, stickety, slickety slam!
> Wallybaloo! Billybazoo!
> We are the boys for a hullabaloo—Western City!"

It sounded all the more deafening, because Bertie, in the front seat, had joined in.

"Hello!" said I. "We must have won the ball-game!"

"You *bet* we did!" said Bertie, in his voice of bursting self-importance.

"Ball-game?" asked Carpenter.

"Foot-ball," said I. "Western City played Union Tech today. Wonder what the score was."

The cheer leader seemed to take the words out of my mouth. Again the hundred voices roared:

> "What was the score?
> Seventeen to four!
> Who got it in the neck?
> Union Tech!
> Who took the kitty?
> Western City!"

Then more waving of flags, and yells for our prize captain and our agile quarter-back: "Rah, rah, rah, Jerry Wilson! Rah, rah, rah, Harriman! Western City, Western City, Western City! W-E-S-T-E-R-N-C-I-T-Y! Western City!"

You have heard college yells, no doubt, and can imagine the tempo of these cries, the cumulative rush of the spelled out letters, the booming roar at the end. The voice of Bertie beat back from the wind-shield with devastating effect upon our ears; and then our car rolled on, and the clamor died away, and I answered the questions of Carpenter. "They are College boys. They have won a game with another college, and are celebrating the victory."

"But," said the other, "how do they manage to shout all together that way?"

"Oh, they've practiced that, of course."

"You mean—they gather and practice making those noises?"

"Surely."

"They make them in cold blood?"

I laughed. "Well, the blood of youth is seldom entirely cold. They imagine the victory while they rehearse, no doubt."

When Carpenter spoke again, it was half to himself. "You make your children into mobs! You train them for it!"

"It really isn't that bad," I replied. "It's all in good temper—it's their play."

"Yes, yes! But what is play but practice for reality? And how shall love be learned in savage war-dances?"

They tell us that we have a new generation of young people since the war; a generation which thinks for itself, and has its own way. I was an advocate of this idea in the abstract, but I must admit that I was startled by the concrete case which I now encountered. Bertie suddenly looked round from his place in the driver's seat. "Say," he demanded, in a grating voice, "where was that guy raised?"

"Bertie *dear!*" cried his mother. "Don't be rude!"

"I'm not being rude," replied the other. "I just want to know where he got his nut ideas."

"Bertie *dear!*" cried the mother, again; and you knew that for eighteen or nineteen years she had been crying "Bertie *dear!*"—in a tone in which rebuke was tempered by fatuous maternal admiration. And all the time, Bertie had gone on doing what he pleased, knowing that in her secret heart his mother was smiling with admiration of his masterfulness, taking it as one more symptom of the greatness of the Stebbins line. I could see him in early childhood, stamping on the floor and commanding his governess to bring him a handkerchief—and throwing his shoe at her when she delayed!

Presently it was Luanda's turn. Lucinda, you understand, was in revolt against the social indignity which her mother had inflicted upon her. When Carpenter had entered the car, she had looked at him once, with a deliberate stare, then lifted her chin, ignoring my effort to introduce him to her. Since then she had sat silent, cold, and proud. But now she spoke. "Mother, tell me, do we have to meet those horrid fat old Jews again?"

Mrs. Stebbins wisely decided that this was not a good time to explore the soul of a possible Eastern potentate. Instead, she elected to talk for a minute or two about a lawn fete she was planning to give next week for the benefit of the Polish relief. "Poland is the World's Bulwark against Bolshevism," she explained; and then added: "Bertie *dear*, aren't you driving recklessly?"

Bertie turned his head. "Didn't you hear me tell that old sheeny I was going to beat him to it?"

"But, Bertie *dear*, this street is crowded!"

"Well, let them look out for themselves!"

But a few seconds later it appeared as if the son and heir of the Stebbins family had decided to take his mother's advice. The car suddenly slowed up—so suddenly as to slide us out of our seats. There was a grinding of brakes, and a bump of something under the wheels; then a wild stream from the sidewalk, and a half-stifled cry from the chauffeur. Mrs. Stebbins gasped, "Oh, my God!" and put her hands over her face; and Lucinda exclaimed, in outraged irritation, "Mamma!" Carpenter looked at me, puzzled, and asked, "What is the matter?"

XX

THE accident had happened in an ill-chosen neighborhood: one of those crowded slum quarters, swarming with Mexicans and Italians and other foreigners. Of course, that was the only neighborhood in which it could have happened, because it is only there that children run wild in the streets at night. There was one child under the front wheels, crushed almost in half, so that you could not bear to look at it, to say nothing of touching it; and there was another, struck by the fender and knocked into the gutter. There was an old hag of a woman standing by, with her hands lifted into the air, shrieking in such a voice of mingled terror and fury as I had never heard in my life before. It roused the whole quarter; there were people running out of twenty houses, I think, before one of us could get out of the car.

The first person out was Carpenter. He took one glance at the form under the car, and saw there was no hope there; then he ran to the child in the gutter and caught it into his arms. The poor people who rushed to the scene found him sitting on the curb, gazing into the pitiful, quivering little face, and whispering grief-stricken words. There was a street-lamp near, so he could see the face of the child, and the crowd could see him.

There came a woman, apparently the mother of the dead child. She saw the form under the car, and gave a horrified scream, and fell into a faint. There came a man, the father, no doubt, and other relatives; there was a clamoring, frantic throng, swarming about the car and about the victims. I went to Carpenter, and asked, "Is it dead?" He answered, "It will live, I think." Then, seeing that the crowd was likely to stifle the little one, he rose. "Where does this child live?" he asked, and some one pointed out the house, and he carried his burden into it. I followed him, and it was fortunate that I did so, because of the part I was able to play.

I saw him lay the child upon a couch, and put his hands upon its forehead, and close his eyes, apparently in prayer. Then, noting the clamor outside growing louder, I went to the door and looked out, and found the Stebbins family in a frightful predicament. The mob had dragged Bertie and the chauffeur outside the car, and were yelling menaces and imprecations into their faces; poor Bertie was shouting back, that it wasn't his fault, how could *he* help it? But they thought he might have helped coming into their quarter with his big rich car; why couldn't he stay in his own part of the city, and kill the children of the rich? A man hit him a blow in the face and knocked him over; his mother shrieked, and leaped out to help him, and half a dozen women flung themselves at her, and as many men at the chauffeur. There was a pile of bricks lying handy, and no doubt also knives in the pockets of these foreign men; I believe the little party would have been torn to pieces, had it not occurred to me to run into the house and summon Carpenter.

Why did I do it? I think because I had seen how the crowd gave way before him with the child in his arms. Anyhow, I knew that I could do nothing alone, and before I could find a policeman it might be many times too late. I told

Carpenter what was happening, and he rose, and ran out to the street.

It was like magic, of course. To these poor foreigners, Catholics most of them, he did not suggest a moving picture actor on location; he suggested something serious and miraculous. He called to the crowd, stretching out his arms, and they gave way before him, and he walked into them, and when he got to the struggling group he held his arms over them, and that was all there was to it.

Except, of course, that he made them a speech. Seeing that he was saving Bertie Stebbins' life, it was no more than fair that he should have his own way, and that a member of the younger generation should listen in unprotesting silence to a discourse, the political and sociological implications of which must have been very offensive to him. And Bertie listened; I think he would not have made a sound, even if he could have, after the crack in the face he had got.

"My people," said Carpenter, "what good would it do you to kill these wretches? The blood-suckers who drain the life of the poor are not to be killed by blows. There are too many of them, and more of them grow in place of those who die. And what is worse, if you kill them, you destroy in yourselves that which makes you better than they, which gives you the right to life. You destroy those virtues of patience and charity, which are the jewels of the poor, and make them princes in the kingdom of love. Let us guard our crown of pity, and not acquire the vices of our oppressors. Let us grow in wisdom, and find ways to put an end to the world's enslavement, without the degradation of our own hearts. For so many ages we have been patient, let us wait but a little longer, and find the true way! Oh, my people, my beloved poor, not in violence, but in solidarity, in brotherhood, lies the way! Let us bid the rich go on, to the sure damnation which awaits them. Let us not soil our hands with their blood!"

He spread out his arms again, majestically. "Stand back! Make way for them!"

Not all the crowd understood the words, but enough of them did, and set the example. In dead silence they withdrew from the sides and front of the car. The body of the dead child had been dragged out of the way and laid on the sidewalk, covered by a coat; and so Carpenter said to the Stebbins family: "The road is clear before you. Step in." Half dazed, the four people obeyed, and again Carpenter raised his voice. "Drinkers of human blood, devourers of human bodies, go your way! Go forward to that doom which history prepares for parasites!"

The engine began to purr, and the car began to move. There was a low mutter from the crowd, a moan of fury and baffled desire; but not a hand was lifted, and the car shot away, and disappeared down the street, leaving Carpenter standing on the curb, making a Socialist speech to a mob of greasers and dagoes.

XXI

WHEN he stopped speaking, it was because a woman pressed her way through the crowd, and caught one of his hands. "Master, my baby!" she sobbed. "The little one that was hurt!" So Carpenter said to the crowd, "The sick child needs me. I must go in." They started to press after him, and he added, "You must not come into the room. The child will need air." He went inside, and knelt once more by the couch, and put his hand on the little one's forehead. The mother, a frail, dark Mexican woman, crouched at the foot, not daring to touch either the man or the child, but staring from one to the other, pressing her hands together in an agony of dread.

The little one opened his eyes, and gazed up. Evidently he liked what he saw, for he kept on gazing, and a smile spread over his features, a wistful and tender and infinitely sad little smile, of a child who perhaps never had a good meal in his lifetime. "Nice man!" he whispered; and the woman, hearing his voice again, began sobbing wildly, and caught Carpenter's free hand and covered it with her tears. "It is all right," said he; "all right, all right! He will get well—do not be afraid." He smiled back at the child, saying: "It is better now; you will not have so much pain." To me he remarked, "What is there so lovely as a child?"

The people thronging the doorway spread word what was going on, and there were shouts of excitement, and presently the voice of a woman, clamoring for admission. The throng made way, and she brought a bundle in her arms, which being unfolded proved to contain a sick baby. I never knew what was the matter with it; I don't suppose the mother knew, nor did Carpenter seem to care. The woman knelt at his feet, praying to him; but he bade her stand up, and took the child from her, and looked into its face, and then closed his eyes in prayer. When he handed back the burden, a few minutes later, she gazed at it. Something had happened, or at least she thought it had happened, for she gave a cry of joy, and fell at Carpenter's feet again, and caught the hem of his garment with one hand and began to kiss it. The rumor spread outside, and there were more people clamoring. Before long, filtering into the room, came the lame, and the halt, and the blind.

I had been reading not long ago of the miracles of Lourdes, so I knew in a general way what to expect. I know that modern science vindicates these things, demonstrating that any powerful stimulus given to the unconscious can awaken new vital impulses, and heal not merely the hysterical and neurotic, but sometimes actual physical ailments. Of course, to these ignorant Mexicans and Italians, there was no possible excitement so great as that caused by Carpenter's appearance and behavior. I understood the thing clearly; and yet, somehow, I could not watch it without being startled—thrilled in a strange, uncomfortable way.

And later on I had company in these unaccustomed emotions; the crowd gave way, and who should come into the room but Mary Magna! She did not speak to either of us, but slipped to one side and stood in silence—while the crowd watched her furtively out of the corner of its eyes, thinking her some foreign princess, with her bold, dark beauty and her costly attire. I went over to her, whispering, "How did you get here?" She explained that, when we did not arrive at the studios, she had called up the Stebbins home and learned about the accident. "They warned me not to come here, because this man was a terrible Bolshevik; he made a blood-thirsty speech to the mob. What did he say?"

I started to tell; but I was interrupted by a piercing shriek. A sick and emaciated young girl with paralyzed limbs had been carried into the room. They had laid her on the couch, from which the child had been taken away, and Carpenter had put his hands upon her. At once the girl had risen up—and here she stood, her hands flung into the air, literally screaming her triumphant joy. Of course the crowd took it up—these primitive people are always glad of a chance to make a big noise, so the whole room was in a clamor, and Carpenter had hard work to extract himself from the throng which wished to touch his hands and his clothing, and to worship him on their knees.

He came over to us, and smiled. "Is not this better than acting, Mary?"

"Yes, surely—if one can do it."

Said he: "Everyone could do it, if they knew."

"Is that really true?" she asked, with passionate earnestness.

"There is a god in every man, and in every woman."

"Why don't they know it, then?"

"There is a god, and also a beast. The beast is old, and familiar, and powerful; the god is new, and strange, and afraid. Because of his fear, the beast kills him."

"What is the beast?"

"His name is self; and he has many forms. In men he is greed; in women he is vanity, and goes attired in much raiment—the chains, and the bracelets, and the mufflers—"

"Oh, don't!" cried Mary, wildly.

"Very well, Mary; I won't." And he didn't. But, looking at Mary, it seemed that she was just as unhappy as if he had.

He turned to an old man who had hobbled into the room on crutches. "Poor old comrade! Poor old friend!" His voice seemed to break with pity. "They have worked you like an old mule, until your skin is cracked and your joints grown hard; but they have not been so kind to you as to an old mule—they have left you to suffer!"

To a pale young woman who staggered towards him, coughing, he cried: "What can I do for you? They are starving you to death! You need food—and I have no food to give!" He raised his arms, in sudden wrath. "Bring forth the masters of this city, who starve the poor, while they themselves riot in wantonness!"

But the members of the Chamber of Commerce and of the Bankers' Association of Western City were not within hearing, nor are their numbers as a rule to be found in the telephone book. Carpenter looked about the place, now lined pretty well with cripples and invalids. Only a couple of hours of spreading rumor had been needed to bring them forth, unholy and dreadful secrets, dragged from the dark corners and back alley-ways of these tenements. He gazed from one crooked and distorted face to another, and put his hand to his forehead with a gesture of despair. "No, no!" he said. "It is of no use!" He lifted his voice, calling once more to the masters of the city. "You make them faster than I can heal them! You make them by machinery—and he who would help them must break the machine!"

He turned to me; and I was startled, for it was as if he had been inside my mind. "I know, it will not be easy! But remember, I broke the empire of Rome!"

That was his last flare. "I can do no more," he whispered. "My power is gone from me; I must rest." And his voice gave way. "I beg you to go, unhappy poor of the world! I have done all that I can do for you tonight."

And silently, patiently, as creatures accustomed to the voice of doom, the sick and the crippled began to hobble and crawl from the room.

XXII

HE sat on the edge of the couch, gazing into space, lost in tragic thought; and Mary and I sat watching him, not quite certain whether we ought to withdraw with the rest. But he did not seem aware of our presence, so we stayed.

In our world it is not considered permissible for people to remain in company without talking. If the talk lags, we have to cast hurriedly about in our minds for something to say—it is called "making conversation." But Carpenter evidently did not know about this custom, and neither of us instructed him. Once or twice I stole a glance at Mary, marvelling at her. All her life she had been a conversational volcano, in a state of perpetual eruption; but now, apparently she passed judgment on her own remarks, and found them not worth making.

In the doorway of the room appeared the little boy who had been knocked down by the car. He looked at Carpenter, and then came towards him. When Carpenter saw him, a smile of welcome came upon his face; he stretched out an arm, and the little fellow nestled in it. Other children appeared in the doorway, and soon he had a group about him, sitting on his knees and on the couch. They were little gutter-urchins, but he, seemingly, was interested in knowing their names and their relationships, what they learned in school, and what games they played. I think he had Bertie's foot-ball crowd in mind, for he said: "Some day they will teach you games of love and friendship, instead of rivalry and strife."

Presently the mother of the household appeared. She was distressed, because it did not seem possible that a great man should be interested in the prattle of children, when he had people like us, evidently rich people, to talk to. "You will bother the master," she said, in Spanish. He seemed to understand, and answered, "Let the children stay with me. They teach me that the world might be happy."

So the prattle went on, and the woman stood in the doorway, with other women behind her, all beaming with delight. They had known all their lives there was something especially remarkable about these children; and here was their pride confirmed! When the little ones laughed, and the stranger laughed with them, you should have seen the pleasure shining from a doorway full of dusky Mexican faces!

But after a while one of the children began to rub his eyes, and the mother exclaimed—it was so late! The children had stayed awake because of the excitement, but now they must go to bed. She bundled them out of the room, and presently came back, bearing a glass of milk and a plate with bread and an orange on it. The master might be hungry, she said, with a humble little bow. In her halting English she offered to bring something to us, but she did not suppose we would care for poor people's food. She took it for granted that "poor people's food" was what Carpenter would want; and apparently she was right, for he ate it with relish. Meantime he tried to get the woman to sit on the couch beside him; but she would not sit in his presence—or was it in the presence of Mary and me? I had a feeling, as she withdrew, that she might have been glad to chat with him, if a million-dollar movie queen and a spoiled young club man had not been there to claim prior rights.

XXIII

SO presently we three were alone once more; and Mary, gazing intently with those big dark eyes that the public knows so well, opened up: "Tell me, Mr. Carpenter! Have you ever been in love?"

I was startled, but if Carpenter was, he gave no sign. "Mary," he said, "I have been in grief." Then thinking, perhaps, that he had been abrupt, he added: "You, Mary—you have been in love?"

She answered: "No." I'm not sure if I said anything out loud, but my thought was easy to read, and she turned upon me. "You don't know what love is. But a woman knows, even though she doesn't act it."

"Well, of course," I replied; "if you want to go into metaphysics—"

"Metaphysics be damned!" said Mary, and turned again to Carpenter.

Said he: "A good woman like you—"

"*Me?*" cried Mary. And she laughed, a wild laugh. "Don't hit me when you've got me down! I've sold myself for every job I ever got; I sold myself for every jewel you saw on me this afternoon. You notice I've got them off now!"

"I don't understand, Mary," he said, gently. "Why does a woman like you sell herself?"

"What else has she got? I was a rat in a tenement. I could have been a drudge, but I wasn't made for that. I sold myself for a job in a store, and then for ribbons to be pretty, and then for a place in the chorus, and then for a speaking part—so on all the way. Now I portray other women selling themselves. They get fancy prices, and so do I, and that makes me a 'star.' I hope you'll never see my pictures."

I sat watching this scene, marvelling more than ever. That tone in Mary Magna's voice was a new one to me; perhaps she had not used it since she played her last "speaking part!" I thought to myself, there was a crisis impending in the screen industry.

Said Carpenter: "What are you going to do about it, Mary?"

"What can I do? My contract has seven years to run."

"Couldn't you do something honest? I mean, couldn't you tell an honest story in your pictures?"

"Me? My God! Tell that to T-S, and watch his face! Why, they hunt all the world over for some new kind of clothes for me to take off; they search all history for some war I can cause, some empire I can wreck. Me play an honest woman? The public would call it a joke, and the screen people would call it indecent."

Carpenter got up, and began to pace the room. "Mary," said he, "I once lived under the Roman empire—"

"Yes, I know. I was Cleopatra, and again I was Nero's mistress while he watched the city burning."

"Rome was rough, and crude, and poor, Mary. Rome was nothing to this. This is Satan on my Father's throne, making new worlds for himself." He paced the room again, then turned and said: "I don't understand this world. I must know more about it, if I am to save it!" There was such grief, such selfless pity in his voijce as he repeated this: "I must know more!"

"You know everything!" exclaimed Mary, suddenly. "You are all wisdom!"

But he went on, speaking as if to himself, pondering his problem: "To serve others, yet not to indulge them; for the cause of their enslavment is that they have accepted service without return. And how shall one preach patience to the poor, when the masters make such preaching a new means of enslavement?" He looked at me, as if he thought that I could answer his question. Then with sudden energy he exclaimed: "I must meet those who are in rebellion against enslavement! Tomorrow I want to meet the strikers—all the strikers in your city."

"You'll have your hands full," I said—for I was a coward, and wanted to keep him out of it.

"How shall I find them?" he persisted.

"I don't know; I suppose their headquarters are at the Labor Temple."

"I will go there. Meantime, I fear I shall have to be alone. I need to think about the things I have learned."

"Where are you going to stay?"

"I don't know."

Said Mary, hesitatingly: "My car is outside—"

He answered: "In ancient days I saw the young patricians drive through the streets in their chariots; no, I shall not ride with them again."

Said I: "I have an apartment at the club, with plenty of room—"

"No, no, friend. I have seen enough of the masters of this city. From now on, if you want to see me, you will find me among the poor."

"If I may meet you in the morning," I said—"to show you to the Labor Temple—" Yes, I would see him through!

"By all means," said he. "But you must come early, for I cannot delay."

"Where shall I come?"

"Come here. I am sure these people will give me shelter." He looked about him. "I suspect that some of them sleep in this room; but they have a little porch outside, and if they will let me stay there I shall be alone, which is what I want now." After a moment, he added, "What I wish to do is to pray. Have you ever tried prayer, Mary?"

She answered, simply, "I wouldn't know how."

"Come to me, and I will teach you," he said.

XXIV

I went early next morning, but not early enough. The Mexican woman told me that "the master" had waited, and finally had gone. He had asked the way to the Labor Temple, and left word that I would find him there. So I stepped back into my taxi, and told the driver to take the most direct route.

Meantime I kept watch for my friend, and I did not have to watch very long. There was a crowd ahead, the street was blocked, and a premonition came to me: "Good Lord, I'm too late—he's got into some new mess!" I leaned out of the window, and sure enough, there he was standing on the tail-end of a truck, haranguing a crowd which packed the street from one line of houses to the other. "And before he got half way to the Labor Temple!" I thought to myself.

I got out, and paid the driver of the taxi, and pushed into the crowd. Now and then I caught a few words of what Carpenter was telling them, and it seemed quite harmless—that they were all brothers, that they should love one another, and not do one another injustice. What could there have been that made him think it necessary to deliver this message before breakfast? I looked about, noting that it was the Hebrew quarter of the city, plastered with signs with queer, spattered-up letters. I thought: "Holy smoke! Is he going to convert the Jews?"

I pushed my way farther into the crowd, and saw a policeman, and went up to him. "Officer, what's this all about?" I spoke as one wearing the latest cut of clothes, and he answered accordingly. "Search me! They brought us out on a riot call, but when we got here, it seems to have turned into a revival meeting."

I got part of the story from this policeman, and part from a couple of bystanders. It appeared that some Jewish lady, getting her shopping done early, had complained of getting short weight, and the butcher had ordered her out of his shop, and she had stopped to express her opinion of profiteers, and he had thrown her out, and she had stood on the sidewalk and shrieked until all the ladies in this crowded quarter had joined her. Their fury against soaring prices and wages that never kept up with them, had burst all bounds, and they had set out to clean up the butcher-shop with the butcher. So there was Carpenter, on his way to the Labor Temple, with another mob to quell!

"You know how it is," said the policeman. "It really does cost these poor devils a lot to live, and they say prices are going down, but I can't see it anywhere but in the papers."

"Well," said I, "I guess you were glad enough to have somebody do this job."

He grinned. "You bet! I've tackled crowds of women before this, and you don't like to hit them, but they claw into your face if you don't. I guess the captain will let this bird spout for a bit, even if he does block the traffic."

We listened for a minute. "Bear in mind, my friends, I am come among you; and I shall not desert you. I give you my justice, I give you my freedom. Your cause is my cause, world without end. Amen."

"Now wouldn't that jar you?" remarked the "copper." "Holy Christ, if you'd hear some of the nuts we have to listen to on street-corners! What do you suppose that guy thinks he can do, dressed up in Abraham's nightshirt?"

Said Carpenter: "The days of the exploiter are numbered. The thrones of the mighty are tottering, and the earth shall belong to them that labor. He that toils not, neither shall he eat, and they that grow fat upon the blood of the people—they shall grow lean again."

"Now what do you think o' that?" demanded the guardian of authority. "If that ain't regular Bolsheviki talk, then I'm dopy. I'll bet the captain don't stand much more of that."

Fortunately the captain's endurance was not put to the test. The orator had reached the climax of his eloquence. "The kingdom of righteousness is at hand. The word will be spoken, the way will be made clear. Meantime, my people, I bid you go your way in peace. Let there be no more disturbance, to bring upon you the contempt of those who do not understand your troubles, nor share the heartbreak of the poor. My people, take my peace with you!" He stretched out his arms in invocation, and there was a murmur of applause, and the crowd began slowly to disperse.

Which seemed to remind my friend the policeman that he had authority to exercise. He began to poke his stick into the humped backs of poor Jewish tailors, and into the ample stomachs of fat Jewish housewives. "Come on now, get along with you, and let somebody else have a bit o' the street." I pushed my way forward, by virtue of my good clothes, and got through the press about Carpenter, and took him by the arm, saying, "Come on now, let's see if we can't get to the Labor Temple."

XXV

THERE was a crowd following us, of course; and I sought to keep Carpenter busy in conversation, to indicate that the crowd was not wanted. But before we had gone half a block I felt some one touch me on the arm, and heard a voice, saying, "I beg pardon, I'm a reporter for the 'Evening Blare'."

Now, of course, I had known this must come; I had realized that I would be getting myself in for it, if I went to join Carpenter that morning. I had planned to warn him, to explain to him what our newspapers are; but how could I have foreseen that he was going to get into a riot before breakfast, and bring out the police reserves and the police reporters?

"Excuse us," I said, coldly. "We have something urgent—"

"I just want to get something of this gentleman's speech—"

"We are on our way to the Labor Temple. If you will come there in a couple of hours, we will give you an interview."

"But I must have a story for our first edition, that goes to press before that."

I had Carpenter by the arm, and kept him firmly walking. I could not get rid of the reporter, but I was resolved to get my warning spoken, regardless of anything. Said I: "This is a matter extremely urgent for you to understand, Mr. Carpenter. This young man represents a newspaper, and anything you say to him will be read in the course of a few hours by perhaps a hundred thousand people. If it is found especially senational, the Continental Press may put it on its wires, and it will go to several hundred papers all over the country—"

"Twelve hundred and thirty-seven papers," corrected the young man.

"So you see, it is necessary that you should be careful what you say—far more so than if you were speaking to a handful of Mexican laborers or Jewish housewives."

Said Carpenter: "I don't understand what you mean. When I speak, I speak the truth."

"Yes, of course," I replied—and meantime I was racking my poor wits figuring out how to present this strange acquaintance of mine most tactfully to the world. I knew the reporter would not tarry long; he would grab a few sentences, and rush away to telephone them in.

"I'll tell you what I'm free to tell," I began. "This gentleman is a healer, a man of very remarkable gifts. Mental healing, you understand."

"I get you," said the reporter. "Some religion?"

"Mr. Carpenter teaches a new religion."

"I see. A sort of prophet! And where does he come from?"

I tried to evade. "He has just arrived—"

But the blood-hound of the press was not going to be evaded. "Where do you come from, sir?" he demanded, of Carpenter.

To which Carpenter answered, promptly: "From God."

"From God? Er—oh, I see. From God! Most interesting! How long ago, may I ask?"

"Yesterday."

"Oh! That is indeed extraordinary! And this mob that you've just been addressing—did you use some kind of mind cure on them?"

I could see the story taking shape; the headlines flamed before my mind's eye—streamer heads, all the way across the sheet, after the fashion of our evening papers:

PROPHET FRESH FROM GOD QUELLS MOB

XXVI

I came to a sudden decision in this crisis. The sensible thing to do was to meet the issue boldly, and take the job of launching Carpenter under proper auspices. He really was a wonderful man, and deserved to be treated decently.

I addressed the reporter again. "Listen. This gentleman is a man of remarkable gifts, and does not take money for them; so, if you are going to tell about him at all, do it in a dignified way."

"Of course! I had no other idea—"

"Your city editor might have another idea," I remarked, drily. "Permit me to introduce myself." I gave him my name, and saw him start.

"You mean *the* Mr.—" Then, giving me a swift glance, he decided it was not necessary to complete the question.

Said I: "Here is my card," and handed it to him.

He glanced at it, and said, "I'll be very glad to explain matters to the desk, and see that the story is handled exactly as you wish."

"Thank you," I replied. "Now, yesterday I was caught in that mob at the picture theatre, and knocked nearly insensible. This gentleman found me, and healed me almost instantly. Naturally, I am grateful, and as I find that he is a teacher, who aids the poor, and will not take money from anyone, I want to thank him publicly, and help to make him known."

"Of course, of course!" said the reporter; and before my mind's eye flashed a new set of headlines:

WEALTHY CLUBMAN MIRACULOUSLY HEALED

Or perhaps it would be a double head:

CLUBMAN, SLUGGED BY MOB, HEALED BY PROPHET

WEALTHY SCION, VICTIM OF PICTURE RIOT, RESTORED BY MAN FRESH FROM GOD

I thought that was sensation enough, and that the interview would end; but alas for my hopes! Said that blood-hound of the press: "Will you give public healings to the people, Mr. Carpenter?"

To which Carpenter answered: "I am not interested in giving healings."

"What? Why not?"

"Worldly and corrupt people ask me to do miracles, to prove my power to them. But the proof I bring to the world is a new vision and a new hope."

"Oh, I see! Your religion! May I ask about it?"

"You are the first; the world will follow you. Say to the people that I have come to understand the nature and causes of their mobs."

"Mobs?" said the puzzled young blood-hound.

"I wish to understand a land which is governed by mobs; I wish to know, who lives upon the madness of others."

"You have been studying a mob this morning?" inquired the reporter.

"I ask, why do the police of Mobland put down the mobs of the poor, and not the mobs of the rich? I ask, who pays the police, and who pays the mobs."

"I see! You are some kind of radical!" And with sickness of soul I saw another headline before my mind's eye:

WEALTHY CLUBMAN AIDS BOLSHEVIK PROPHET

I hastened to break in: "Mr. Carpenter is not a radical; he is a lover of man." But then I realized, that did not sound just right. How the devil was I to describe this man? How came it that all the phrases of brotherhood and love had come to be tainted with "radicalism"? I tried again: "He is a friend of peace."

"Oh, really!" observed the reporter. "A pacifist, hey?" And I thought: "Damn the hound!" I knew, of course, that he had the rest of the formula in his head: "Pro-German!" Out loud I said: "He teaches brotherhood."

But the hound was not interested in my generalities and evasions. "Where have you seen mobs of the rich, Mr. Carpenter?"

"I have seen them whirling through the streets in automobiles, killing the children of the poor."

"You have seen that?"

"I saw it last night."

Now, I had inspected our "Times" and our "Examiner" that morning, and noted that both, in their accounts of the accident, had given only the name of the chauffeur, and suppressed that of the owner. I understood what an amount of social and financial pressure that feat had taken; and here was Carpenter about to spoil it! I laid my hand on his arm, saying: "My friend, you were a guest in that car. You are not at liberty to talk about it."

I expected to be argued with; but Carpenter apparently conceded my point, for he fell silent. It was the young reporter who spoke. "You were in an auto accident, I judge? We had only one report of a death, and that was caused by Mrs. Stebbins' car. Were you in that?" Then, as neither Carpenter nor I replied, he laughed. "It doesn't matter, because I couldn't use the story. Mr. Stebbins is one of our 'sacred cows.' Good-day, and thank you."

He started away; and suddenly all my terror of newspaper publicity overwhelmed me. I simply could not face the public as guardian of a Bolshevik! I shouted: "Young man!" And the reporter turned, respectfully, to listen. "I tell you, Mr. Carpenter is *not* a radical! Get that clear!" And to the young man's skeptical half-smile I exclaimed: "He's a Christian!" At which the reporter laughed out loud.

XXVII

WE got to the Labor Temple, and found the place in a buzz of excitement, over what had occurred in front of Prince's last night. I had suspected rough work on the part of the police, and here was the living evidence—men with bandages over cracked heads, men pulling open their shirts or pulling up their sleeves to show black and blue bruises. In the headquarters of the Restaurant Workers we found a crowd, jabbering in a dozen languages about their troubles; we learned that there were eight in jail, and several in the hospital, one not expected to live. All that had been going on, while we sat at table gluttonizing—and while tears were running down Carpenter's cheeks!

It seemed to me that every third man in the crowd had one of the morning's newspapers in his hand—the newspapers which told how a furious mob of armed ruffians had sought to break its way into Prince's, and had with difficulty been driven off by the gallant protectors of the law. A man would read some passage which struck him as especially false; he would tell what he had seen or done, and he would crumple the paper in his hand and cry. "The liars! The dirty liars!"—adding adjectives not suitable for print.

I realized more than ever that I had made a mistake in letting Carpenter get into this place. It was no resort for anybody who wanted to be patriotic, or happy about the world. All sorts of wonderful promises had been made to labor, to persuade it to win the war; and now labor came with the blank check, duly filled out according to its fancy—and was in process of being kicked downstairs. Wages were being "liquidated," as the phrase had it; and there was an endless succession of futile strikes, all pitiful failures. You must understand that Western City is the home of the "open shop;" the poor devils who went on strike were locked out of the factories, and slugged off the streets; their organizations were betrayed by spies, and their policies dedeviled by provocateurs. And all the mass of misery resulting seemed to have crowded into one building this bright November morning; pitiful figures, men and women and even a few children— for some had been turned out of their homes, and had no place to go; ragged, haggard, and underfed; weeping, some of them, with pain, or lifting their clenched hands in a passion of impotent fury. My friend T-S, the king of the movies, with all his resources, could not have made a more complete picture of human misery—nor one more fitted to work on the sensitive soul of a prophet, and persuade him that capitalist America was worse than imperial Rome.

The arrival of Carpenter attracted no particular attention. The troubles of these people were too recent for them to be aware of anything else. All they wanted was some one to tell their troubles to, and they quickly found that this stranger was available for the purpose. He asked many questions, and before long had a crowd about him—as if he were some sort of government commissioner, conducting an investigation. It was an all day job, apparently; I hung round, trying to keep myself inconspicuous.

Towards noon came a boy with newspapers, and I bought the early edition of the "Evening Blare." Yes, there it was—all the way across the front page; not even a big fire at the harbor and an earthquake in Japan had been able to displace it. As I had foreseen, the reporter had played up the most sensational aspects of the matter: Carpenter announced himself as a prophet only twenty-four hours out of God's presence, and proved it by healing the lame and the halt and the blind—and also by hypnotising everyone he spoke to, from a wealthy young clubman to a mob of Jewish housewives. Incidentally he denounced America as "Mobland," and called it a country governed by madmen.

I took the paper to him, thinking to teach him a little worldly prudence. Said I: "You remember, I tried to keep out that stuff about mobs—"

He took the sheet from my hands and looked at the headlines. I saw his nostrils dilate, and his eyes flash. "Mobs? This paper is a mob! It is the worst of your mobs!" And it fell to the floor, and he put his foot on the flaring print.

Said he: "You talk about mobs—listen to this." Then, to one of the group about him: "Tell how they mobbed you!" The man thus addressed, a little Russian tailor named Korwsky, narrated in his halting English that he was the secretary of the tailors' union, and they had a strike, and a few days ago their offices had been raided at night, the door "jimmed" open and the desk rifled of all the papers and records. Evidently it had been done by the bosses or their agents, for nothing had been taken but papers which would be of use against the strike. "Dey got our members' list," said Korwsky. "Dey send people to frighten 'em back to verk! Dey call loans, dey git girls fired from stores if dey got jobs—dey hound 'em every way!"

The speaker went on to declare that no such job could have been pulled off without the police knowing; yet they made no move to arrest the criminals. His voice trembled with indignation; and Carpenter turned to me.

"You have mobs that come at night, with dark lanterns and burglars' tools!"

I had noticed among the men talking to Carpenter one who bore a striking resemblance to him. He was tall and not too well nourished; but instead of the prophet's robes of white and amethyst, he wore the clothes of a working-man, a little too short in the sleeves; and where Carpenter had a soft and silky brown beard, this man had a skinny Adam's apple that worked up and down. He was something of an agitator, I judged, and he appeared to have a religious streak. "I am a Christian," I heard him say; "but one of the kind that speak out against injustice. And I can show you Bible texts for it," he insisted. "I can prove it by the word of God."

This man's name was James, and I learned that he was one of the striking carpenters. The prophet turned to him, and said: "Tell him your story." So the other took from his pocket a greasy note-book, and produced a newspaper clipping, quoting an injunction which Judge Wollcott had issued against his union. "Read that," said he; but I answered that I knew about it. I remember hearing my uncle laughing over the matter at the dinner-table, saying that "Bobbie" Wollcott had forbidden the strikers to do everything but sit on air and walk on water. And now I got another view of "Bobbie," this time from a prophet fresh from God. Said the prophet: "Your judges are mobs!"

XXVIII

SOON after the noon-hour, there pushed his way into the crowd a young man, whom I recognized as one of the secretaries of T-S. He was looking for me, and told me in a whisper that his employer was downstairs in his car, and wanted to see Mr. Carpenter and myself about something important. He did not want to come up, because it was too conspicuous. Would we come down and take a little drive? I answered that I should be willing, but I knew Carpenter would not—he had been in an automobile accident the night before, and had refused to ride again.

Then, said the secretary, was there some room where we could meet? I went to one of the officials, and asked for a vacant room where I could talk about a private matter with a friend. I managed to separate Carpenter from his crowd and took him to the room, and presently Everett, the secretary, came with T-S.

The great man shook hands cordially with both of us; then, looking round to make sure that no one heard us, he began: "Mr. Carpenter, I told you I vould give a tousand dollars to dese strikers."

The other's face, which had looked so grey and haggard, was suddenly illumined as if by his magical halo. "I had forgotten it! There are so many hungry in there; I have been watching them, wondering when they would be fed."

"All right," said T-S. "Here you are." And reaching into his pocket, he produced a wad of new shiny hundred dollar notes, folded together. "Count 'em."

Carpenter took the money in his hand. "So this is it!" he said. He looked at it, as if he were inspecting some strange creature from the wilds of Patagonia.

"It's de real stuff," said T-S, with a grin.

"The stuff for which men sell their souls, and women their virtue! For which you starve and beat and torture one another—"

"Ain't it pretty?" said the magnate, not a bit embarrassed.

The other began reading the writing on the notes—as you may remember having done in some far-off time of childhood. "Whose picture is this?" he asked.

"I dunno," said the magnate. "De Secretary of de Treasury, I reckon."

"But," said the other, "why not your picture, Mr. T-S?"

"Mine?"

"Of course."

"My picture on de money?"

"Why not? You are the one who makes it, and enables everyone else to make it."

It was one of those brand new ideas that come only to geniuses and children. I could see that T-S had never thought of it before; also, that he found it interesting to think of. Carpenter went on: "If your picture was on it, then every one would know what it meant. People would say: 'Render unto T-S the things that are T-S's.' When you were paying off your mobs, you would pay them with your own money, and whenever they spent it, the people would bow to Caesar—I mean to T-S."

He said it without the trace of a smile; and T-S had no idea there was a smile anywhere in the neighborhood. In a business-like tone he said: "I'll tink about it." Then he went on: "You give it to de strikers—"

But Carpenter interrupted: "It was you who were going to give it. I cannot give nor take money."

"You mean you von't take it to dem?"

"I couldn't possibly do it, Mr. T-S."

"But, man—"

"Your promise was that *you* would come and give it. Now do so."

"But, Mr. Carpenter, if I vas to do such a ting, it vould cost me a million dollars. I vould git into a row vit de Merchants' and Manufacturers' Association, dey vould boycott my business, dey vould give me a black eye all over de country. You dunno vot you're askin', Mr. Carpenter."

"I understand then—you are in business alliance with men who are starving these people into submission, and you are afraid to help them? Afraid to feed the poor!" The far-off, wondering look came again to his face. "The world is organized!" he said, to himself. "There is a mob of masters! What can I do to save the people?"

T-S was unchanged in his cheerful good-nature. "You give dem a tousand dollars and you help a lot. Nobody can do it all."

But Carpenter was not satisfied; he shook his head, sadly. "Please take this," he said, and pressed the roll of bills back into the hands of the astounded magnate!

XXIX

HOWEVER, T-S had come there to get something that day, and I thought I knew what it was. He swallowed his consternation, and all the rest of his emotions. "Now, now, Mr. Carpenter! Ve ain't a-goin' to quarrel about a ting like dat. Dem fellers is hungry, and de money vill give dem vun good feed. Ve git somebody to bring it to dem, and we be friends shoost de same. Billy, maybe you could give it, hey?"

I drew back with a laugh. "You don't get me into your quarrels!"

"Vell," said T-S—and suddenly he had an inspiration. "I know. I git Mary Magna to give it! She's a voman!"

Carpenter turned with sudden wonder. "Then women are permitted to have hearts?"

"Shoost so, Mr. Carpenter! Ha, ha, ha! Ve business fellers—my Gawd, if you knew vot business is, you'd vunder we got hearts enough to keep our blood movin'."

"Business," said Carpenter, still pondering. "Then it's business—"

"Yes, business—" put in T-S. "Dat's it!" And he lowered his voice, and looked round once more. "It's time we vas talkin' business now! Mr. Carpenter, I be frank vit you, I put all my cards on de table. I seen de papers shoost now, vot vunderful tings you do—healin' de sick and quellin' de mobs and all dat— and I tink I gotta raise my offer, Mr. Carpenter. If you sign a contract I got here in my pocket, I pay you a tousand dollars a veek. Vot you say, my friend?"

Carpenter did not say anything, and so the magnate began to expatiate upon the artistic triumphs he would achieve. "I make such a picture fer you as de vorld never seen before. You can do shoost vot you vant in dat story—all de tings you like to do, and nuttin' you didn't like. I never said dat to no man before, but I know you now, Mr. Carpenter, and all I ask you is to heal de sick and quell de mobs, shoost like today. I pledge you my vord—I put it in de contract if you say so—I make nuttin' but Bible pictures."

"That is very kind of you, Mr. T-S, and I thank you for the compliment; but I fear you will have to get some one else to play my part."

Said T-S: "I vant you to tink, Mr. Carpenter, vot it vould mean if you had a tousand dollars every week. You could feed all de babies of de strikers. I vouldn't care vot you did—you could feed my own strikers, ven I git some at Eternal City. A tousand dollars a veek is an awful pile o' money to have!"

"I know that, my friend."

"And vot's more, I pay you five tousand cash on de signin' of de contract. You can go right in now vit dese strikers—maybe you could beat Prince's vit all dat money!" Then, as Carpenter still shook his head: "I give you vun more raise, my friend—but dat's de last, you gotta believe me. I pay you fifteen hunded a veek. I aint ever paid so much money to a green actor in my life before, and I don't tink anybody else in de business ever did."

But still Carpenter shook his head!

"Vould you mind tellin' me vy, Mr. Carpenter?"

"Not at all. You tell me that I may quell mobs for you. But there are mobs in your business that I could not quell."

"Vot mobs?"

"Among others, yourself."

"Me?"

"Yes—you are a mob; a mob of money! You storm the souls of men, and of women too. It will take a stronger force than I to quell you."

"I don't git you," said T-S, helplessly; but then, thinking it over a bit, he went on: "I guess I'm a vulgar feller, Mr. Carpenter, and maybe all my pictures ain't vot you call high-brow. But if I had a man like you to vork vit, I could make vot you call real educational pictures. You're vot dey call a prophet, you got a message fer de vorld; vell, vy don't you let me spread it fer you? If you use my machinery, you can talk to a billion people. Dat's no joke—if dey is dat many alive, I bring 'em to you; I bring de Japs and de Chinks and de niggers—de vooly-headed savages vot vould eat your missionaries if you sent 'em. I offer you de whole vorld, Mr. Carpenter; and you vould be de boss!"

Carpenter became suddenly grave. "My friend," said he, "a long time ago there was a prophet, and he was offered the world. The story is told us—'Again, the devil taketh him up into an exceeding high mountain, and sheweth him all the kingdoms of the world, and the glory of them; and saith unto him, All these things will I give thee, if thou wilt fall down and worship me.' You recall that story, Mr. T-S?"

"No," said T-S, "I ain't vun o' dese litry fellers." But he realized that the story was not complimentary to him, and he showed his chagrin. "I tell you vun ting, Mr. Carpenter, if you vas to know me better, you vouldn't call me a devil."

And suddenly the other put his hand on the great man's shoulder. "I believe that, my friend; I hate the sin but love the sinner—And so, suppose you come to lunch with me?"

"Lunch?" said T-S, taken aback.

"I went to dinner with you last night. Now you come to lunch with me."

"Vere at, Mr. Carpenter?"

Said Carpenter: "When I went with you, I did not ask where."

Carpenter signed to me and to Everett, the secretary, and the four of us went out of the room. I was as much mystified as the picture magnate, but I held my peace, and Carpenter led us to the elevator, and down to the street. "No," said he, to T-S, "there is no need to get into your car. The place is just around the corner." And he put his arm in that of the magnate, and led him down the street—somewhat to the embarrassment of his victim, for there was a crowd following us. People had read the afternoon papers by now, and it was no longer possible to walk along unheeded, with a prophet only twenty-four hours from God, who healed the sick and quelled mobs before breakfast. But T-S set his teeth and bore it—hoping this might be the way to land his contract.

XXX

WE turned the corner, and soon I saw what was before us, and almost cried out with glee. It was really too good to be true! Carpenter, in the course of his talks with strikers, had learned where their soup-kitchen was located, the relief-headquarters where their families were being fed; and he now had the sublime audacity to take the picture magnate to lunch among them!

The place was an empty warehouse, fitted with long tables, and benches made of planks that were old and full of splinters. Here in rows of twenty or thirty were seated men and women and children, mixed together; before each one a bowl of not very thick soup, and a hunk of bread, and a tin cup full of hot brown liquid, politely taken for coffee. It was a meal which would have been spurned by any of the "studio bums" of T-S's mob-scenes; but now T-S was going to be a good sport, and sit on a splintery plank and eat it!

Nor was that all. As we pushed our way into the place, Carpenter turned to the magnate, and without a trace of embarrassment, said: "You understand, Mr. T-S, I have no money. But we must pay—"

"Oh, sure!" said T-S, quickly. "I'll pay!"

"Thank you," said the other; and he turned to an official of the union with whom he had got acquainted in the course of the morning. He introduced us all, not forgetting the secretary, and then said: "Mr. T-S is the moving picture producer, and wants to have lunch with you, if you will consent."

"Oh, sure!" said the official, cordially.

"He will pay for it," added Carpenter. "He has brought along a thousand dollars for that purpose."

T-S started as if some one had struck him; and the official started too. "WHAT?"

"He will pay a thousand dollars," declared Carpenter. "It is a fact, and you may tell the people, if you wish."

"My Gawd, no!" cried T-S wildly.

But the official did not heed him. He faced the crowd and stretched out his arms. "Boys! Boys! This is Mr. T-S, the picture producer, and he's come to lunch with us, and he's going to pay a thousand dollars for it!"

There was a moment of amazed silence, then a roar from the company. Men leaped to their feet and yelled. And there stood poor T-S-not enjoying the ovation!

"Give it to them," whispered Carpenter; and the magnate, thus held up, took out the roll of bills, and turned it over to the trembling official, who leaped onto a chair and waved the miracle before the crowd. "A thousand dollars! A thousand dollars!" He counted it over before their eyes and called, louder than ever, "A thousand dollars!"

Carpenter, followed by T-S and the secretary and myself, went down the line of tables, shaking hands with many on the way, and being patted on the back by others. Also T-S shook hands, and was patted. Seats were found for us, and food was brought—double portions of it, as if to make the plight of the poor magnate even more absurd! I watched him out of the corner of my eye; he enjoyed that costly meal just about as much as Carpenter had enjoyed the one at Prince's last night!

However, he was game, and spilled no tears into his soup; and Carpenter ate with honest appetite, having had no breakfast. The strikers about us ate as if they had missed both breakfast and supper; they laughed and chatted and made jokes with us—you would have thought they were celebrating the winning of the strike and the end of all their troubles. In the midst of the meal I noted two well-dressed young men by the door, asking questions; I chuckled to myself, seeing more head-lines—double ones, and extra size:

PROPHET OF GOD VAMPS MOVIE KING MAGNATE OF SCREEN
PAYS THOUSAND FOR LUNCH

But I knew that T-S had never yet paid a thousand dollars without getting something for it, and I was not surprised when, after he had gulped down his meal, he turned to his host and, disregarding the company and the excitement, demanded, "Now, Mr. Carpenter, tell me, do I git de contract?"

Carpenter had had his jest, and was through with it. He answered, gravely: "You must understand me, Mr. T-S. You don't want a contract with me."

"I don't?"

"If I were to sign it, it would not be a week before you would be sorry, and would be asking me to release you."

"Vy is dat, Mr. Carpenter?"

"Because I am going to do things which will make me quite useless to you in a business way."

"Dat can't be true, Mr. Carpenter!"

"It is true, and you will realize it soon. I assure you, it won't be a day before you will be ashamed of having known me."

T-S was gazing at the speaker, not certain whether this was something very terrible, or only a polite evasion. "Mr. Carpenter," he answered, "if all de vorld vas to give you up, I vouldn't!"

Said Carpenter: "I tell you, before the cock crows again, you will deny three times that you know me." And then, without awaiting response from the amazed T-S, he turned to speak to the man on the other side of him.

The magnate of the pictures sat silent, evidently frightened. At last he turned to me and asked, "Vot you tink he meant by dat, Billy?"

I answered: "I think he meant that you are to play the part of Peter."

"Peter? Peter Pan?"

"No; St. Peter, who denied his master."

"Veil," said T-S, patiently, "you know, I ain't vun o' dese litry fellers."

"I'll tell it to you some time," I continued. "It's kind of funny. If he's right, you are going to be the first pope, and sit at the golden gate, holding the keys of heaven."

"My Gawd!" said T-S.

"And you've made a record in the movies." I added. "You've played Satan and St. Peter, both on the same day! That is 'doubling' with a vengeance!"

XXXI

WHEN I got back to the Labor Temple, I learned that there was to be a mass-meeting of the strikers this Saturday evening. It had been planned some days ago, and now was to be turned into a protest against police violence and "government by injunction." There was a cheap afternoon paper which professed sympathy with the workers, and this published a manifesto, signed by a number of labor leaders, summoning their followers to make clear that they would no longer submit to "Cossack rule."

It appeared now that these leaders were considering inviting Carpenter to become one of the speakers at their meeting. Two of them came up to me. I had heard this stranger speak, and did I think he could hold an audience? I gave assurance; he was a man of dignity, and would do them credit. They were afraid the newspapers would represent him as a freak, but of course their meeting would hardly fare very well in the papers anyhow. One of them asked, cautiously, how much of an extremist was he? Labor leaders were having a hard time these days to hold down the "reds," and the employers were not giving them any help. Did I think Carpenter would support the "reds"? I answered that I didn't know the labor movement well enough to judge, but one thing they could be sure of, he was a man of peace, and would not preach any sort of violence.

The matter was settled a little later, when Mary Magna drove up to the Labor Temple in her big limousine. Mary, for the first time in the memory of anyone who knew her, was without her war-paint; dressed like a Quakeress—a most uncanny phenomenon! She had not a single jewel on; and before long I learned why—she had taken all she owned to a jeweler that morning, and sold them for something over six thousand dollars. She brought the money to the fund for the babies of the strikers; nor did she ask anyone else to hand it in for her. It was Mary's fashion to look the world in the eye and say what she was doing.

T-S was still hanging about, and at first he tried to check this insane extravagance, but then he thought it over and grinned, saying, "I git my tousand dollars back in advertising!" When I pointed out to him what would be the interpretation placed by newspaper gossip on Mary's intervention in the affairs of Carpenter, he grinned still more widely. "Ain't he got a right to be in love vit Mary? All de vorld's in love vit Mary!" And of course, there was a newspaper reporter standing by his side, so that this remark went out to the world as semi-official comment!

You understand that by this time the second edition of the papers was on the streets, and it was known that the new prophet was at the Labor Temple. Curiosity seekers came filtering in, among them half a dozen more reporters, and as many camera men. After that, poor Carpenter could get no peace at all. Would he please say if he was going to do any more healing? Would he turn a little more to the light—just one second, thank you. Would he mind making a group with Miss Magna and Mr. T-S and the "wealthy young scion"? Would he consent to step outside for some moving pictures, before the light got too dim? It was a new kind of mob—a ravening one, making all dignity and thought impossible. In the end I had to mount guard and fight the publicity-hounds away. Was it likely this man would go out and pose for cameras, when he had just refused fifteen hundred dollars a week from Mr. T-S to do that very thing? And then more excitement! Had he really refused such an offer? The king of the movies admitted that he had!

We live in an age of communication; we can send a bit of news half way round the world in a few seconds, we can make it known to a whole city in a few hours. And so it was with this "prophet fresh from God"; in spite of himself, he was seized by the scruff of the neck and flung up to the pinnacle of fame! He had all the marvels of a lifetime crowded into one day—enough to fill a whole newspaper with headlines!

And the end was not yet. Suddenly there was a commotion in the crowd, and a man pushed his way through—Korwsky, the secretary of the tailor's union, who, learning of Carpenter's miracles, had rushed all the way home, and got a friend with a delivery wagon, and brought his half-grown son post-haste. He bore him now in his arms, and poured out to Carpenter the pitiful tale of his paralyzed limbs. Such a gentle, good child he was; no one ever heard a complaint; but he had not been able to stand up for five years.

So, of course, Carpenter put his hands upon the child, and closed his eyes in prayer; and suddenly he put him down to the ground and cried: "Walk!" The lad stared at him, for one wild moment, while people caught their breath; then, with a little choking cry, he took a step. There came a shout from the spectators, and then—Bang!—a puff as if a gun had gone off, and a flash of light, and clouds of white smoke rolling to the ceiling.

Women screamed, and one or two threatened to faint; but it was nothing more dangerous than the cameraman of the Independent Press Service, who had hired a step-ladder, and got it set up in a corner of the room, ready for any climax! A fine piece of stage management, said his jealous rivals; others in the crowd were sure it was a put up job between Carpenter and Korwsky. But the labor leaders knew the little tailor, and they believed. After that there was no doubt about Carpenter's being a speaker at the mass-meeting!

XXXII

IT came time when the rest of us were ready for dinner, but Carpenter said that he wanted to pray. Apparently, whenever he was tired, and had work to do he prayed. He told me that he would find his own way to Grant Hall, the place of the mass-meeting; but somehow, I didn't like the idea of his walking through the streets alone. I said I would call for him at seven-thirty and made him promise not to leave the Labor Temple until that hour.

I cast about in my mind for a body-guard, and bethought me of old Joe. His name is Joseph Camper, and he played centre-rush with my elder brother in the days before they opened up the game, and when beef was what counted. Old Joe has shoulders like the biggest hams in a butcher shop, and you can trust him like a Newfoundland dog. I knew that if I asked him not to let anybody hurt my friend, he wouldn't—and this regardless of the circumstance of my friend's not wearing pants. Old Joe knows nothing about religion or sociology— only wrestling and motor-cars, and the price of wholesale stationery.

So I phoned him to meet me, and we had dinner, and at seven-thirty sharp our taxi crew drew up at the Labor Temple. Half a minute later, who should come walking down the street but Everett, T-S's secretary! "I thought I'd take the liberty," he said, apologetically. "I thought Mr. Carpenter might say something worth while, and you'd be glad to have a transcript of his speech."

"Why, that's very kind of you," I answered, "I didn't know you were interested in him."

"Well, I didn't know it myself, but I seem to be; and besides, he told me to follow him."

I went upstairs, and found the stranger waiting in the room where I had left him. I put myself on one side of him, and the ex-centre-rush on the other, with Everett respectfully bringing up the rear, and so we walked to Grant Hall. Many people stared at us, and a few followed, but no one said anything—and thank God, there was nothing resembling a mob! I took my prophet to the stage entrance of the hall, and got him into the wings; and there was a pathetically earnest lady waiting to give him a tract on the horrors of vivisection, and an old gentleman with a white beard and palsied hands, inviting him to a spiritualistic seance. Funniest of all, there was Aunt Caroline's prophet, the author of the "Eternal Bible," with his white robes and his permanent wave, and his little tribute of carrots and onions wrapped in a newspaper. I decided that these were Carpenter's own kind of troubles, and I left him to attend to them, and strolled out to have a look at the audience.

The hall was packed, both the floor and the galleries; there must have been three thousand people. I noted a big squad of police, and wondered what was coming; for in these days you can never tell whether any public meeting is to be allowed to start, and still less if it is to be allowed to finish. However, the crowd was orderly, the only disturber being some kind of a Socialist trying to sell literature.

I saw Mary Magna come in, with Laura Lee, another picture actress, and

Mrs. T-S. They found seats; and I looked for the magnate, and saw him talking to some one near the door. I strolled back to speak to him, and recognized the other man as Westerly, secretary of the Merchants' and Manufacturers' Association. I knew what he was there for—to size up this new disturber Of the city's peace, and perhaps to give the police their orders.

It was not my wish to overhear the conversation, but it worked out that way, partly because it is hard not to overhear T-S, and partly because I stopped in surprise at the first words: "Good Gawd, Mr. Vesterly, vy should I vant to give money to strikers? Dat's nuttin' but fool newspaper talk. I vent to see de man, because Mary Magna told me he vas a vunderful type, and I said I'd pay him a tousand dollars on de contract. You know vot de newspapers do vit such tings!"

"Then the man isn't a friend of yours?" said the other.

"My Gawd, do I make friends vit every feller vot I hire because he looks like a character part?"

At this point there came up Rankin, one of T-S's directors. "Hello!" said he. "I thought I'd come to hear your friend the prophet."

"Friend?" said T-S. "Who told you he's a friend o' mine?"

"Why, the papers said—"

"Vell, de papers 're nutty!"

And then came one of the strikers who had been in the soup-kitchen—a fresh young fellow, proud to know a great man. "How dy'do, Mr. T-S? I hear our friend, Mr. Carpenter, is going—"

"Cut out dis friend stuff!" cried T-S, irritably. "He may be yours—he ain't mine!"

I strolled up. "Hello, T-S!" I said.

"Oh, Billy! Hello!"

"So you've denied him three times!"

"Vot you mean?"

"Three times—and the cock hasn't crowed yet! That man's a prophet for sure, T-S!"

The magnate pretended not to understand, but the deep flush on his features gave him away.

"How dy'do, Mr. Westerly," I said. "What do you think of Mr. T-S in the role of the first pope?"

"You mean he's going to act?" inquired the other, puzzled.

"Come off!" exclaimed Rankin, who knew better, of course.

"He's going to be St. Peter," I insisted, "and hold the keys to the golden gate. He's planning a religious play, you know, for this fellow Carpenter. Maybe he might cast Mr. Westerly for a part—say Pontius Pilate."

"Ha, ha, ha!" said the secretary of our "M. and M." "Pretty good! Ha, ha, ha! Gimme a chance at these bunk-shooters—I'll shut 'em up, you bet!"

XXXIII

THE chairman of the meeting was a man named Brown, the president of the city's labor council. He was certainly respectable enough, prosy and solemn. But he was deeply moved on this question of clubbing strikers' heads; and you could see that the crowd was only waiting for a chance to shout its indignation. The chairman introduced the president of the Restaurant Workers, a solid citizen whom you would have taken for a successful grocer. He told about what had happened last night at Prince's; and then he told about the causes of the strike, and the things that go on behind the scenes in big restaurants. I had been to Prince's many times in my life, but I had never been behind the scenes, nor had I ever before been to a labor-meeting. I must admit that I was startled. The things they put into the hashes! And the distressing habit of unorganized waiters, when robbed of their tips or otherwise ill-treated, to take it out by spitting into the soup!

A couple of other labor men spoke, and then came James, the carpenter with a religious streak. He had a harsh, rasping voice, and a way of poking a long bony finger at the people he was impressing. He was desperately in earnest, and it caused him to swallow a great deal, and each time his Adam's apple would jump up. "I'm going to read you a newspaper clipping," he began; and I thought it was Judge Wollcott's injunction again, but it was a story about one of our social leaders, Mrs. Alinson Pakenham, who has four famous Pekinese spaniels, worth six thousand dollars each, and weighing only eight ounces—or is it eighty ounces?—I'm not sure, for I never was trusted to lift one of the wretched little brutes. Anyhow, their names are Fe, Fi, Fo, and Fum, and they have each their own attendant, and the four have a private limousine in which to travel, and they dine off a service of gold plate. And here were hundreds of starving strikers, with their wives, also starving; and a couple of thousand other workers in factories and on ranches who were in process of having their wages "deflated." The orator quoted a speech of Algernon de Wiggs before the Chamber of Commerce, declaring that the restoration of prosperity, especially in agriculture, depended upon "deflation," and this alone; and suddenly James, the carpenter with a religious streak, launched forth:

"Go to now, you rich men, weep and howl for your miseries that are coming upon you! Your riches are corrupted, and your garments are moth-eaten! Your gold and silver is cankered; and the rust on it shall be a witness against you, and shall eat your flesh as if it were fire. You have heaped treasure together for the last days. Behold the hire of the laborers, who have reaped your fields; you have kept it back by fraud, and the cries of the reapers have entered into the ears of the Lord! You have lived in pleasure on the earth, and been wanton; you have nourished your hearts, as in a day of slaughter. You have condemned and killed the just—"

At this point in the tirade, my old friend the ex-centre-rush, who was standing in the wings with me, turned and whispered: "For God's sake, Billy, what kind of a Goddamn Bolshevik stunt is this, anyhow?"

I answered: "Hush, you dub! He's quoting from the Bible!"

XXXIV

PRESIDENT Brown of the Western City Labor Council arose to perform his next duty as chairman. Said he:

"The next speaker is a stranger to most of you, and he is also a stranger to me. I do not know what his doctrine is, and I assume no responsibility for it. But he is a man who has proven his friendship for labor, not by words, but by very unusual deeds. He is a man of remarkable personality, and we have asked him to make what suggestions he can as to our problems. I have pleasure in introducing Mr. Carpenter."

Whereupon the prophet fresh from God arose from his chair, and come slowly to the front of the platform. There was no applause, but a silence made part of curiosity and part of amazement. His figure, standing thus apart, was majestic; and I noted a curious thing—a shining as of light about his head. It was so clear and so beautiful that I whispered to Old Joe: "Do you see that halo?"

"Go on, Billy!" said the ex-centre-rush. "You're getting nutty!"

"But it's plain as day, man!"

I felt some one touch my arm, and saw the little lady of the anti-vivisection tracts peering past me. "Do you see his aura?" she whispered, excitedly.

"Is that what it is?"

"Yes. It's purple. That denotes spirituality."

I thought to myself, "Good Lord, am I getting to be that sort?"

Carpenter began to speak, quietly, in his grave, measured voice. "My brothers!" He waited for some time, as if that were enough; as if all the problems of life would be solved, if only men would understand those two words. "My brothers: I am, as your chairman says, a stranger to this world of yours. I do not understand your vast machines and your complex arts. But I know the souls of men and women; when I meet greed, and pride, and cruelty, the enslavements of the flesh, they cannot lie to me. And I have walked about the streets of your city, and I know myself in the presence of a people wandering in a wilderness. My children!—broken-hearted, desolate, and betrayed—poorest when you are rich, loneliest when you throng together, proudest when you are most ignorant—my people, I call you into the way of salvation!"

He stretched out his arms to them, and on his face and in his whole look was such anguish, that I think there was no man in that whole great throng so rooted in self-esteem that he was not shaken with sudden awe. The prophet raised his hands in invocation: "Let us pray!" He bowed his head, and many in the audience did the same. Others stared at him in bewilderment, having long ago forgotten how to pray. Here and there some one snickered.

"Oh, God, Our Father, we, Thy lost children, return to Thee, the Giver of Life. We bring our follies and our greeds, and cast them at Thy feet. We do not like the life we have lived. We wish to be those things which for long ages we have dreamed in vain. Wilt Thou show the way?"

His hands sank to his sides, and he raised his head. "Such is the prayer.

What is the answer? It has been made known: Ask, and it shall be given you; seek, and ye shall find; knock, and it shall be opened unto you. For everyone that asketh receiveth; and he that seeketh findeth; and to him that knocketh it shall be opened.—These are ancient words, by many forgotten. What do they mean? They mean that we are children of our Father, and not slaves of earthly masters. Would a man make a slave of his own child? And shall man be more righteous than his Creator?

"My brothers: You are hungry, and in need, and your children cry for bread; do I bid you feed them upon words? Not so; but the life of men is made by the will of men, and that which exists in steel and stone existed first in thought. If your thought is mean and base, your world is a place of torment; if your thought is true and generous, your world is free.

"There was once a man who owned much land, and upon it he built great factories, and many thousand men toiled for him, and he grew fat upon the product of their labor, and his heart was high. And it came to pass that his workers rebelled; and he hired others, and they shot down the workers, so that the rest returned to their labor. And the master said: The world is mine, and none can oppose me. But one day there arose among the workers a man who laughed. And his laughter spread, until all the thousands were laughing; they said, We are laughing at the thought that we should work and you take the fruit of our labor. He ordered his troops to shoot them, but his troops were also laughing, and he could not withstand the laughter of so many men; he laughed also, and said, let us end this foolish thing.

"Is there a man among you who can say, I am worthy of freedom? That man shall save the world. And I say to you: Make ready your hearts for brotherhood; for the hour draws near, and it is a shameful thing when man is not worthy of his destiny. A man may serve with his body, and yet be free, but he that is a slave in his soul admires the symbols of mastery, and lusts after its fruits.

"What are the fruits of mastery? They are pride and pomp, they are luxury and wantoness and the shows of power. And who is there among you that can say to himself, these things have no roots in my heart? That man is great, and the deliverance of the world is the act of his will."

XXXV

THE speaker paused, and turned; his gaze swept the platform, and those seated on it. Said he: "You are the representatives of organized labor. I do not know your organization, therefore I ask: For what are you united? Is it to follow in the footsteps of your masters, and bind others as they have bound you?"

He waited for an answer, and the chairman, upon whom his gaze was fixed, cried, "No!" Others also cried, "No!" and the audience took it up with fervor. Carpenter turned to them. "Then I say to you: Break down in your hearts and in the hearts of your fellows the worship of those base things which mastership has brought into the world. If a man pile up food while others starve, is not this evil? If a woman deck herself with clothing to her own discomfort, is not this folly? And if it be folly, how shall it be admired by you, to whom it brings starvation and despair?

"Before me sit young women of the working class. Say to yourselves: I tear from my fingers the jewels which are the blood and tears of my fellow-men; I wash the paint from my face, and from my head and my bosom I take the silly feathers and ribbons. I dare to be what I am. I dare to speak truth in a world of lies. I dare to deal honestly with men and women.

"Before me sit young men of the working-class. I say to you: Love honest women. Do not love harlots, nor imitations of harlots. Do not admire the idle women of the ruling class, nor those who ape them, and thereby glorify them. Do not admire languid limbs and pouting lips and the signs of haughtiness and vanity, your own enslavements.

"A tree is known by the fruit it gives; and the masters are known by the lives they give to their servants. They are known by misery and unemployment, by plague and famine, by wars, and the slaughter of the people. Let judgment be pronounced upon them!

"You have heard it said: Each for himself, and the devil take the hindmost. But I say to you: Each for all, and the hindmost is your charge. I say to you: If a man will not work, let him be the one that hungers; if he will not serve, let him be your criminal. For if one man be idle, another man has been robbed; and if any man make display of wealth, that man has the flesh of his brothers in his stomach. Verily, he that lives at ease while others starve has blood-guilt upon him; and he that despises his fellows has committed the sin for which there is no pardon. He that lives for his own glory is a wolf, and vengeance will hunt him down; but he that loves justice and mercy, and labors for these things, dwells in the bosom of my Father.

"Do not think that I am come to bring you ease and comfort; I am come to bring strife and discontent to this world. For the time of martyrdom draws near, and from your Father alone can you draw the strength to endure your trials. You are hungry, but you will be starved; you are prisoned in mills and mines, but you will be walled up in dungeons; you are beaten with whips, but you will be beaten with clubs, your flesh will be torn by bullets, your skin will be burned with fire and your lungs poisoned with deadly gases—such is the dominion of this world.

But I say to you, resist in your hearts, and none can conquer you, for in the hearts of men lies the past and the future, and there is no power but love.

"You say: The world is evil, and men are base; why should I die for them? Oh, ye of little faith, how many have died for you, and would you cheat mankind? If there is to be goodness in the world, some one must begin; who will begin with me?

"My brothers: I am come to lead you into the way of justice. I bid you follow; not in passion and blind excitement, but as men firm in heart and bent upon service. For the way of self-love is easy, while the way of justice is hard. But some will follow, and their numbers will grow; for the lives of men have grown ill beyond enduring, and there must be a new birth of the spirit. Think upon my message; I shall speak to you again, and the compulsion of my law will rest upon you. The powers of this world come to an end, but the power of good will is everlasting, and the body can sooner escape from its own shadow than mankind can escape from brotherhood."

He ceased, and a strange thing happened. Half the crowd rose to its feet; and they cried, "Go, on!" Twice he tried to retire to his seat, but they cried, "Go on, go on!" Said he, "My brothers, this is not my meeting, there are other speakers—" But they cried, "We want to hear you!" He answered, "You have your policies to decide, and your leaders must have their say. But I will speak to you again to-morrow. I am told that your city permits street speaking on Western City Street on Sundays. In the morning I am going to church, to see how they worship my Father in this city of many mobs; but at noon I will hold a meeting on the corner of Fifth and Western City Streets, and if you wish, you may hear me. Now I ask you to excuse me, for I am weary." He stood for a moment, and I saw that, although he had never raised his voice nor made a violent gesture, his eyes were dark and hollow with fatigue, and drops of sweat stood upon his forehead.

He turned and left the platform, and Old Joe and I hurried around to join him. We found him with Korwsky the little Russian tailor whose son he had healed. Korwsky claimed him to spend the night at his home; the friend with the delivery wagon was on hand, and they were ready to start. I asked Carpenter to what church he was going in the morning, and he startled me by the reply, "St. Bartholomew's." I promised that I would surely be on hand, and then Old Joe and I set out to walk home.

"Well?" said I. "What do you think of him?"

The ex-centre-rush walked for a bit before he answered. "You know, Billy boy," said he, "we do lead rotten useless lives."

"Good Lord!" I thought; it was the first sign of a soul I had ever noted in Old Joe! "Why," I argued, "you sell paper, and that's useful, isn't it?"

"I don't know whether it is or not. Look at what's printed on it—mostly advertisements and bunk." And again we walked for a bit. "By the way," said the ex-centre-rush, "before he got through, I saw that aura, or whatever you call it. I guess I'm getting nutty, too!"

XXXVI

THE first thing I did on Sunday morning was to pick up the "Western City Times," to see what it had done to Carpenter. I found that he had achieved the front page, triple column, with streamer head all the way across the page:

PROPHET IN TOWN, HEALS SICK, RAVES AT RICH AMERICA IS MOBLAND, ALLEGED IN RED RIOT OF TALK

There followed a half page story about Carpenter's strenuous day in Western City, beginning with a "Bolshevik stump speech" to a mob of striking tailors. It appears that the prophet had gone to the Hebrew quarter of the city, and finding a woman railing at a butcher because of "alleged extortion," had begun a speech, inciting a mob, so that the police reserves had to be called out, and a riot was narrowly averted. From there the prophet had gone to the Labor Temple, announcing himself to the reporters as "fresh from God," with a message to "Mobland," his name for what he prophesied America would be under his rule. He had then healed a sick boy, the performance being carefully staged in front of moving picture cameras. The account of the "Times" did not directly charge that the performance was a "movie stunt," but it described it in a mocking way which made it obviously that. The paper mentioned T-S in such a way as to indicate him as the originator of the scheme, and it had fun with Mary Magna, pawning her paste jewels. It published the flash-light picture, and also a picture of Carpenter walking down the street, trailed by his mob.

In another column was the climax, the "red riot of talk" at Grant Hall. James, the striking carpenter, had indulged in virulent and semi-insane abuse of the rich; after which the new prophet had stirred the mob to worse frenzies. The "Times" quoted sample sentences, such as: "Do not think that I am come to bring you ease and comfort; I am come to bring strife and disorder to this world."

I turned to the editorial page, and there was a double-column leader, made extra impressive by leads. "AN INFAMOUS BLASPHEMY," was the heading. Perhaps you have a "Times" in your own city; if so, you will no doubt recognize the standard style:

"For many years this newspaper has been pointing out to the people of Western City the accumulating evidence that the men who manipulate the forces of organized labor are Anarchists at heart, plotting to let loose the torch of red revolution over this fair land. We have clearly showed their nefarious purpose to overthrow the Statue of Liberty and set up in its place the Dictatorship of the Walking Delegate. But, evil as we thought them, we were naive enough to give them credit for an elemental sense of decency. Even though they had no respect for the works of man, we thought at least they would spare the works of God, the most sacred symbols of divine revelation to suffering humanity. But yesterday there occurred in this city a performance which for shameless insolence and blasphemous perversion exceeds anything but the wildest flight of a devil's imagination, and reveals the bosses of the Labor Trust as wanton defilers of everything that decent people hold precious and holy.

"What was the spectacle? A moving picture producer, moved by blind, and we trust unthinking lust for gain, produces in our midst an alleged 'prophet,' dressed in a costume elaborately contrived to imitate and suggest a Sacred Presence which our respect for religion forbids us to name; he brings this vile, perverted creature forward, announcing himself to the newspapers as 'fresh from God,' and mouthing phrases of social greed and jealousy with which for the past few years the Hun-agents and Hun-lovers in our midst have made us only too sickenly familiar. This monstrous parody of divine compassion is escorted to that headquarters of Pro-Germanism and red revolution, the Labor Temple, and there performs, in the presence of moving picture cameras, a grotesque parody upon the laying on of hands and the healing of the sick. The 'Times' presents a photograph of this incredible infamy. We apologize to our readers for thus aiding the designs of cunning publicity-seekers, but there is no other way to make clear to the public the gross affront to decency which has been perpetrated, and the further affronts which are being planned. This appears to be a scheme for making a moving picture 'star'; this 'Carpenter'—note the silly pun—is to become the latest sensation in million dollar movie dolls, and the American public is to be invited to pay money to witness a story of sacred things played by a real 'prophet' and worker of 'miracles'!"

"But the worst has yet to be told. The masters of the Labor Trust, not to be outdone in bidding for unholy notoriety, had the insolence to invite this blasphemous charlatan to their riot of revolutionary ranting called a 'protest meeting.' He and other creatures of his ilk, summoning the forces which are organizing red ruin in our city, proceed to rave at the police and the courts for denying to mobs of strikers the right to throw brickbats at honest workers looking for jobs, and to hold the pistol of the boycott at the heads of employers who dare to stand for American liberty and democracy! We have heard much mouthing of class venom and hate in this community, but never have our ears been affronted by anything so unpardonable as this disguising of the doctrine of Lenin and Trotsky in the robes of Christian revelation. This 'prophet fresh from God,' as he styles himself, is a man of peace and brotherly love—oh, yes, of course! We know these wolves in sheeps' clothing, these pacifists and lovers of man with the gold of the Red International in their pockets, and slavering from their tongues the fine phrases of idealism which conveniently protect them from the strong hand of the law! We have seen their bloody work for four years in Russia, and we tell them that if they expect to prepare the confiscation of property and the nationalization of women in this country while disguising themselves in moving picture imitations of religion, they are grossly underestimating the intelligence of the red-blooded citizens of this great republic. We shall be much mistaken if the order-loving and patriotic people of our Christian community do not find a way to stamp their heel upon this vile viper before its venom shall have poisoned the air we breathe."

4

XXXVII

THEN I picked up the "Examiner." Our "Examiner" does not go in so much for moral causes; it is more interested in getting circulation, for which it relies upon sensation, and especially what it calls "heart interest," meaning sex. It had found what it wanted in this story, as you may judge by the headlines:

MOVIE QUEEN PAWNS JEWELS FOR PROPHET OF GOD

Then followed a story of which Mary Magna was the centre, with T-S and myself for background. The reporter had hunted out the Mexican family with which Carpenter had spent the night, and he drew a touching picture of Carpenter praying over Mary in this humble home, and converting her to a better life. Would the "million dollar vamp," as the "Examiner" called her, now take to playing only religious parts? Mary was noncommittal on the point; and pending her decision, the "Examiner" published her portraits in half a dozen of her most luxurious roles—for example, as Salome after taking off the seventh veil. Side by side with Carpenter, that had a real "punch," you may believe!

The telephone rang, and there was the voice of T-S, fairly raving. He didn't mind the "Examiner" stuff; that was good business, but that in the "Times"—he was going to sue the "Times" for a million dollars, by God, and would I back him in his claim that he had not put Carpenter up to the healing business?

After a bit, the magnate began apologizing for his repudiation of the prophet. He was in a position, just now with these hard times, where the Wall Street crowd could ruin him if he got in bad with them. And then he told me a curious story. Last night, after the meeting, young Everett, his secretary, had come to him and asked if he could have a couple of months' leave of absence without pay. He was so much interested in Carpenter that he wanted to follow him and help him!

"Y' know, Billy," said the voice over the phone, "y' could a' knocked me over vit a fedder! Dat young feller, he vas alvays so quiet, and such a fine business feller, I put him in charge of all my collections. I said to him, 'Vot you gonna do?' And he said, 'I gonna learn from Mr. Carpenter." Says I, 'Vot you gonna learn?' and he says, 'I gonna learn to be a better man.' Den he vaits a minute, and he says, 'Mr. T-S, he told me to foller him!' J' ever hear de like o' dat?"

"What did you say?"

"Vot could I say? I vanted to say, 'Who's givin' you de orders?' But I couldn't, somehow! I hadda tell him to go ahead, and come back before he forgot all my business."

I dressed, and had my breakfast, and drove to St. Bartholomew's. It was a November morning, bright and sunny, as warm as summer; and it is always such a pleasure to see that goodly company of ladies and gentlemen, so perfectly groomed, so perfectly mannered, breathing a sense of peace and well being. Ah, that wonderful sense of well being! "God's in His Heaven, all's right with the world!" And what a curious contrast with the Labor Temple! For a moment I doubted Carpenter; surely these ladies with their decorative bonnets, their sweet perfumes, their gowns of rose and lilac and other pastel shades—surely they were more important life-products than women in frowsy and dowdy imitation clothes! Surely it was better to be serene and clean and pleasant, than to be terrible and bewildered, sick and quarrelsome! I was seized by a frenzy, a sort of instinctive animal lust for this life of ease and prettiness. No matter if those dirty, raucous-voiced hordes of strikers, and others of their "ilk"—as the "Times" phrased it—did have to wash my clothes and scrub my floors, just so that *I* stayed clean and decent!

I bowed to a score or two of the elegant ladies, and to their escorts in shiny top hats and uncreased kid gloves, and went into the exquisite church with its glowing stained glass window, and looked up over the altar—and there stood Carpenter! I tell you, it gave me a queer shock. There he was, up in the window, exactly where he had always been; I thought I had suddenly wakened from a dream. There had been no "prophet fresh from God," no mass-meeting at Grant Hall, no editorial in the "Times"! But suddenly I heard a voice at my elbow: "Billy, what is this awful thing you've been doing?" It was my Aunt Caroline, and I asked what she meant, and she answered, "That terrible prophet creature, and getting your name into the papers!"

So I knew it was true, and I walked with my dear, sweet old auntie down the aisle, and there sat Aunt Jennie, with her two lanky girls who have grown inches every time I run into them; and also Uncle Timothy. Uncle Timothy was my guardian until I came of age, so I am a little in awe of him, and now I had to listen to his whispered reproaches—it being the first principle of our family never to "get into the papers." I told him that it wasn't my fault I had been knocked down by a mob, and surely I couldn't help it if this man Carpenter found me while I was unconscious, and made me well. Nor could I fail to be polite to my benefactor, and try to help him about. My Uncle Timothy was amazed, because he had accepted the "Times" story that it was all a "movie" hoax. Everybody will tell you in Western City that they "never believe a word they read in the 'Times'"; but of course they do—they have to believe something, and what else have they?

I was trying to think about that picture over the altar. Of course, they would naturally have replaced it! I wondered who had found old de Wiggs up there; I wondered if he knew about it, and if he had any idea who had played that prank. I looked to his pew; yes, there he sat, rosy and beaming, bland as ever! I looked for old Peter Dexter, president of the Dexter Trust Company—yes, he was in his pew, wizened and hunched up, prematurely bald. And Stuyvesant Gunning, of the Fidelity National—they were all here, the masters of the city's finance and the pillars of "law and order." Some wag had remarked if you wanted to call directors' meeting after the service, you could settle all the business of Western City in St. Bartholomew's!

The organ pealed and the white-robed choir marched in, bearing the golden crosses, and followed by the Reverend Dr. Lettuce-Spray, smooth-shaven, plump and beautiful, his eyes bent reverently on the floor. They were singing with fervor that most orthodox of hymns:

The church's one foundation Is Jesus Christ, her Lord.

It is a beautiful old service, as you may know, and I had been taught to love it and thrill to it as a little child, and we never forget those things. Peace and propriety are its keynotes; order and dignity, combined with sensuous charm. Everyone knows his part, and it moves along like a beautiful machine. I knelt and prayed, and then sat and listened, and then stood and sang—over and over for perhaps three-quarters of an hour. We came to the hymn which precedes the sermon, and turning to the number, we obediently proclaimed:

The Son of God goes forth to war A kingly crown to gain: His blood-red banner streams afar: Who follows in His train?

During the singing of the last verse, the Reverend Lettuce-Spray had moved silently into the pulpit. After the choir had sung "Amen," he raised his hands in invocation—and at that awesome moment I saw Carpenter come striding up the aisle!

XXXVIII

HE knew just where he was going, and walked so fast that before anyone had time to realize what was happening, he was on the altar steps, and facing the congregation. You could hear the gasp of amazement; he was so absolutely identical with the painted figure over his head, that if he had remained still, you could not have told which was painting and which was flesh and blood. The rector in the pulpit stood with his mouth open, staring as if seeing a ghost.

The prophet stretched out both his hands, and pointed two accusing fingers at the congregation. His voice rang out, stern and commanding: "Let this mockery cease!" Again he cried: "What do ye with my Name?" And pointing over his head: "Ye crucify me in stained glass!"

There came murmurs from the congregation, the first mutterings of a storm. "Oh! Outrageous! Blasphemy!"

"Blasphemy?" cried Carpenter. "Is it not written that God dwelleth not in temples made with hands? Ye have built a temple to Mammon, and defile the name of my Father therein!"

The storm grew louder. "This is preposterous!" exclaimed my uncle Timothy at my side. And the Reverend Lettuce-Spray managed to find his voice. "Sir, whoever you are, leave this church!"

Carpenter turned upon him. "You give orders to me—you who have brought back the moneychangers into my Father's temple?" And suddenly he faced the congregation, crying in a voice of wrath: "Algernon de Wiggs! Stand up!"

Strange as it may seem, the banker rose in his pew; whether under the spell of Carpenter's majestic presence, or preparing to rush at him and throw him out, I could not be sure. The great banker's face was vivid scarlet.

And Carpenter pointed to another part of the congregation. "Peter Dexter! Stand up!" The president of the Dexter Trust Company also arose, trembling as if with palsy, mumbling something, one could not tell whether protest or apology.

"Stuyvesant Gunning! Stand up!" And the president of the Fidelity National obeyed. Apparently Carpenter proposed to call the whole roll of financial directors; but the procedure was halted suddenly, as a tall, white-robed figure strode from its seat near the choir. Young Sidney Simpkinson, assistant to the rector, went up to Carpenter and took him by the arm.

"Leave this house of God," he commanded.

The other faced him. "It is written, Thou shalt not take the name of the Lord thy God in vain, for the Lord will not hold him guiltless that taketh His name in vain."

Young Simpkinson wasted no further words in parley. He was an advocate of what is known as "muscular Christianity," and kept himself in trim playing on the parish basket-ball team. He flung his strong arms about Carpenter, and half carrying him, half walking him, took him down the steps and down the aisle. As he went, Carpenter was proclaiming: "It is written, My house shall be called a house of prayer; but ye have made it a den of thieves. He that steals little is called a pickpocket, but he that steals much is called a pillar of the church. Verily, he that deprives the laborer of the fruit of his toil is more dangerous than he that robs upon the highway; and he that steals the state and the powers of government is the father of all thieves."

By that time, the prophet had been hustled two-thirds down the aisle; and then came a new development. Unobserved by anyone, a number of Carpenter's followers had come with him into the church; and these, seeing the way he was being handled, set up a cry: "For shame! For shame!" I saw Everett, secretary to T-S, and Korwsky, secretary of the tailor's union; I saw some one leap at Everett and strike him a ferocious blow in the teeth, and two other men leap upon the little Russian and hurl him to the ground.

I started up, involuntarily. "Oh, shame! Shame!" I cried, and would have rushed out into the aisle. But I had to pass my uncle, and he had no intention of letting me make myself a spectacle. He threw his arms about me, and pinned me against the pew in front; and as he is one of the ten ranking golfers at the Western City Country Club, his embrace carried authority. I struggled, but there I stayed, shouting, "For shame! For shame!" and my uncle exclaiming, in a stern whisper, "Shut up! Sit down, you fool!" and my Aunt Caroline holding onto my coat-tails, crying, and my aunt Jennie threatening to faint.

The melee came quickly to an end, for the men of the congregation seized the half dozen disturbers and flung them outside, and mounted guard to make sure they did not return. I sank back into my seat, my worthy uncle holding my arm tightly with both hands, lest I should try to make my escape over the laps of Aunt Caroline and Aunt Jennie.

All this time the Reverend Lettuce-Spray had been standing in the pulpit, making no sound. Now, as the congregation settled back into order, he said, with the splendid, conscious self-possession of one who can remain "equal to the occasion": "We will resume the service." And he opened his portfolio, and spread out his manuscript before him, and announced:

"Our text for the morning is the fifth chapter of the gospel according to St. Matthew, the thirty-ninth and fortieth verses: 'But I say unto you, that ye resist not evil: but whosoever shall smite thee on thy right cheek, turn to him the other also. And if any man shall sue thee at law, and take away thy coat, let him have thy cloak also.'"

XXXIX

I sat through the sermon, and the offertory, and the recessional. After that my uncle tried to detain me, to warn and scold me; but he no longer used physical force, and nothing but that would have held me. At the door I asked one of the ushers what had become of the prophet, thinking he might be in jail. But the answer was that the gang had gone off, carrying their wounded; so I ran round the corner to where my car was parked, and within ten minutes I was on Western City Street, where Carpenter had announced that he would speak.

There had been nothing said about the proposed meeting in the papers, and no one knew about it save those who had been present at Grant Hall. But it looked as if they had told everyone they knew, and everyone they had told had come. The wide street was packed solid for a block, and in the midst of this throng stood Carpenter, upon a wagon, making a speech.

There was no chance to get near, so I bethought me of an alley which ran parallel to the street. There was an obscure hotel on the street, and I entered it through the rear entrance, and had no trouble in persuading the clerk to let me join some of the guests of the hotel who were watching the scene from the second story windows.

The first thing which caught my attention was the figure of Everett, seated on the floor of the wagon from which the speech was being made. I saw that his face was covered with blood; I learned later that he had three teeth knocked out, and his nose broken. Nevertheless, there he was with his stenographer's notebook, taking down the prophet's words. He told me afterwards that he had taken even what Carpenter said in the church. "I've an idea he won't last very long," was the way he put it; "and if they should get rid of him, every word he's said will be precious. Anyhow, I'm going to get what I can."

Also I saw Korwsky, lying on the floor of the wagon, evidently knocked out; and two other men whom I did not know, nursing battered and bloody faces. Having taken all that in at a glance, I gave my attention to what Carpenter was saying.

He was discussing churches and those who attend them. Later on, my attention was called to the curious fact that his discourse was merely a translation into modern American of portions of the twenty-third chapter of St. Matthew; a free adaptation of those ancient words to present day practices and conditions. But I had no idea of this while I listened; I was shocked by what seemed to me a furious tirade, and the guests of the hotel were even more shocked—I think they would have taken to throwing things out of the windows at the orator, had it not been for their fear of the crowd. Said Carpenter:

"The theologians and scholars and the pious laymen fill the leisure class churches, and it would be all right if you were to listen to what they preach, and do that; but don't follow their actions, for they never practice what they preach. They load the backs of the working-classes with crushing burdens, but they themselves never move a finger to carry a burden, and everything they do is for show. They wear frock-coats and silk hats on Sundays, and they sit at the speakers' tables at the banquets of the Civic Federation, and they occupy the best pews in the churches, and their doings are reported in all the papers; they are called leading citizens and pillars of the church. But don't you be called leading citizens, for the only useful man is the man who produces. (Applause.) And whoever exalts himself shall be abased, and whoever humbles himself shall be exalted.

"Woe unto you, doctors of divinity and Catholics, hypocrites! for you shut up the kingdom of heaven against men; you don't go in yourself and you don't let others go in. Woe unto you, doctors of divinity and Presbyterians, hypocrites! for you foreclose mortgages on widows' houses, and for a pretense you make long prayers. For this you will receive the greater damnation! Woe unto you, doctors of divinity and Methodists, hypocrites! for you send missionaries to Africa to make one convert, and when you have made him, is twice as much a child of hell as yourselves. (Applause.) Woe unto you, blind guides, with your subtleties of doctrine, your transubstantiation and consubstantiation and all the rest of it; you fools and blind! Woe unto you, doctors of divity and Episcopalians, hypocrites! for you drop your checks into the collection-plate and you pay no heed to the really important things in the Bible, which are justice and mercy and faith in goodness. You blind guides, who choke over a fly and swallow a flivver! (Laughter.) Woe unto you, doctors of divinity and Anglicans, hypocrites! for you dress in immaculate clothing kept clean by the toil of frail women, but within you are full of extortion and excess. You blind high churchmen, clean first your hearts, so that the clothes you wear may represent you. Woe unto you, doctors of divinity and Baptists, hypocrites! for you are like marble tombs which appear beautiful on the outside, but inside are full of dead men's bones and all uncleanness. Even so you appear righteous to men, but inside you are full of hypocrisy and iniquity. (Applause.) Woe unto you doctors of divinity and Unitarians, hypocrites! because you erect statues to dead reformers, and put wreaths upon the tombs of old-time martyrs. You say, if we had been alive in those days, we would not have helped to kill those good men. That ought to show you how to treat us at present. (Laughter.) But you are the children of those who killed the good men; so go ahead and kill us too! You serpents, you generation of vipers, how can you escape the damnation of hell?"

XL

WHEN Carpenter stopped speaking, his face was dripping with sweat, and he was pale. But the eager crowd would not let him go. They began to ask him questions. There were some who wanted to know what he meant by saying that he came from God, and some who wanted to know whether he believed in the Christian religion. There were others who wanted to know what he thought about political action, and if he really believed that the capitalists would give up without using force. There was a man who had been at the relief kitchen, and noted that he ate soup with meat in it, and asked if this was not using force against one's fellow creatures. The old gentleman who represented spiritualism was on hand, asking if the dead are still alive, and if so, where are they?

Then, before the meeting was over, there came a sick man to be healed; and others, pushing their way through the crowd, clamoring about the wagon, seeking even to touch the hem of Carpenter's garments. After a couple of hours of this he announced that he was worn out. But it was a problem to get the wagon started; they could only move slowly, the driver calling to the people in front to make room. So they went down the street, and I got into my car and followed at a distance. I did not know where they were going, and there was nothing I could do but creep along—a poor little rich boy with a big automobile and nobody to ride in it, or to pay any attention to him.

The wagon drove to the city jail; which rather gave me a start, because I had been thinking that the party might be arrested at any minute, on complaint to the police from the church. But apparently this did not trouble Carpenter. He wished to visit the strikers who had been arrested in front of Prince's restaurant. He and several others stood before the heavy barred doors asking for admission, while a big crowd gathered and stared. I sat watching the scene, with phrases learned in earliest childhood floating through my mind: "I was sick, and ye visited me; I was in prison, and ye came unto me."

But it appeared that Sunday was not visitors' day at the jail, and the little company was turned away. As they climbed back into the wagon, I saw two husky fellows come from the jail, a type one learns to know as plain clothes men. "Why won't they let him in?" cried some one in the crowd; and one of the detectives looked over his shoulder, with a sneering laugh: "We'll let him in before long, don't you worry!"

The wagon took up its slow march again. It was a one-horse express-cart, belonging, as I afterwards learned, to a compatriot of Korwsky the tailor. This man, Simon Karlin, earned a meager living for himself and his family by miscellaneous delivery in his neighborhood; but now he was so fascinated with Carpenter that he had dropped everything in order to carry the prophet about. I mention it, because next day in the newspapers there was much fun made of this imitation man of God riding about town in a half broken-down express-wagon, hauled by a rickety and spavined old nag.

The company drove to one of the poorer quarters of the city, and stopped before a workingman's cottage on a street whose name I had never heard before. I learned that it was the home of James, the striking carpenter, and on the steps were his wife and a brood of half a dozen children, and his old father and mother, and several other people unidentified. There were many who had walked all the way following the wagon, and others gathered quickly, and besought the prophet to speak to them, and to heal their sick. Apparently his whole life was to consist of that kind of thing, for he found it hard to refuse any request. But finally he told them he must be quiet, and went inside, and James mounted guard at the door, and I sat in my car and waited until the crowd had filtered away. There was no good reason why I should have been admitted, but James apparently was glad to see me, and let me join the little company that was gathered in his home.

There was Everett, who had now washed the blood off his face, but had not been able to put back his lost teeth, nor to heal the swollen mass that had once been his upper lip and nose. And there was Korwsky, who was now able to sit up and smile feebly, and two other men, whose names I did not learn, nursing battered faces. Carpenter prayed over them all, and they became more cheerful, and eager to talk about the adventure, each telling over what had happened to him. I noted that Everett, in spite of what must have been intense pain, was still faithfully taking down every word the prophet uttered.

It had been known that Carpenter was to honor this house with his presence, and the family were all dressed in their best, and had got together a supper, in spite of hard times and strikes. We had sandwiches and iced tea and a slice of pie for each of us, and I was interested to observe that the prophet, tired as he was, liked to laugh and chat over his food, exactly like any uninspired human being. He never failed to get the children around him and tell them stories, and hear their bright laughter.

XLI

BUT, of course, serious things kept intruding. Karlin the express driver, had a sick wife, and Carpenter heard about her and insisted upon going to see her. Apparently there was no end to this business of the poor being sick. It was a new thing to me—this world swarming with dirty and miserable and distracted people. Of course, I had known about "the poor," but always either in the abstract, or else as an individual, or a family, that one could help. But here was a new world, thickly peopled, swarming; that was the terrible part of it—the vastness of it, the thickness of the population in these regions of "the poor." It was like some sort of delirium; like being lost in a wilderness, of which the trees were miseries, and deformities, and pains! I could understand to the full Carpenter's feeling when he put his hands to his forehead, exclaiming: "There is so much to do and so few to do it! Pray to God, that he will send some to help us!"

When he returned from Simon Karlin's, he brought with him the latter's wife, whom he had healed of a fever; and here was another of the company whom he insisted upon helping—"Comrade" Abell, one of the men I had noticed at the meeting last night, and who appeared to be done up. This man, I learned, was secretary of the Socialist local of Western City. I had known there were Socialists in the city, just as I knew there were poor, but I had never seen one, and was curious about Abell. He was a lawyer; and that might suggest to you a pertain type of person, brisk and well dressed—but apparently Socialist lawyers are not true to type. Comrade Abell was a shy, timid little man, with black hair straggling about his ears, and sometimes into his eyes. He had a gentle, pathetic face, and his voice was melancholy and caressing. He was clad in a frock coat of black broadcloth, which had once been appropriate for Sunday; but I should judge it had been worn for twenty years, for it was green about the collar and the cuffs and button-holes.

Comrade Abell's office and also his home were in a second story, over a grocery-store in this neighborhood, and here also was a little hall used as a meeting-place by the Socialists. Every Saturday night Abell and two or three of his friends conducted a soap-box meeting on Western City Street, and gave away propaganda leaflets and sold a few pamphlets and books. He had had quite a supply of literature of all kinds at his office, nearly two thousand dollars worth, he told Carpenter, but a few months previously the place had been mobbed. A band of ex-service men, accompanied by a few police and detectives, had raided it and terrified the wife and children by breaking down the doors and throwing the contents of desks and bureaus out on the floor. They had dumped the literature into a truck and carted it away, and after two or three weeks they had dumped it back again, having found nothing criminal in it. "But they ruined it so that it can't be sold!" broke in James, indignantly. "Most of it was bought on credit, and how can we pay for it."

James was also a Socialist, it appeared, while Korwsky and his friend Karlin advocated "industrial action," and these fell to arguing over "tactics," while

Carpenter asked questions, so as to understand their different points of view. Presently Korwsky was called out of the room, and came back with an announcement which he evidently considered grave. John Colver was in the neighborhood, and wanted to know if Carpenter would meet him.

"Who is John Colver?" asked the prophet. And it was explained that this was a dangerous agitator, now under sentence of twenty years in jail, but out on bail pending the appeal of his case to the supreme court. Colver was a "wobbly," well known as one of their poets. Said Korwsky, "He tinks you vouldn't like to know him, because if de spies find it out, dey vould git after you."

"I will meet any man," said Carpenter. "My business is to meet men." And so in a few minutes the terrible John Colver was escorted into the room.

Now, every once in a while I had read in the "Times" how another bunch of these I.W.W's. were put on trial, and how they were insolent to the judge, and how it was proved they had committed many crimes, and how they were sentenced to fourteen years in State's prison under our criminal syndicalism act. Needless to say, I had never seen one of these desperate men; but I had a quite definite idea what they looked like—dark and sinister creatures, with twisted mouths and furtive eyes. I knew that, because I had seen a couple of moving picture shows in which they figured. But now for the first time I met one, and behold, he was an open-faced, laughing lad, with apple cheeks and two most beautiful rows of even white teeth that gleamed at you!

"Fellow-worker Carpenter!" he cried; and caught the prophet by his two hands. "You are an old friend of ours, though you may not know it! We drink a toast to you in our jungles."

"Is that so?" said Carpenter.

"I suppose I really have no right to see you," continued the other, "because I'm shadowed all the time, and you know my organization is outlawed."

"Why is it outlawed?"

"Well," said Colver, "they say we burn crops and barns, and drive copper-nails into fruit-trees, and spikes into sawmill lumber."

"And do you do that?"

Colver laughed his merry laugh. "We do it just as often as you act for the movies, Fellow-worker Carpenter!"

"I see," said Carpenter. "What do you really do?"

"What we really do is to organize the unskilled workers."

"For what do you organize them?"

"So that they will be able to run the industries when the system of greed breaks down of its own rottenness."

"I see," said the prophet, and he thought for a moment. "It is a slave revolt!"

"Exactly," said the other.

"I know what they do to slave revolts, my brother. You are fortunate if they only send you to prison."

"They do plenty more than that," said Colver. "I will give you our pamphlet, 'Drops of Blood,' and you may read about some of the lynching and tarring and feathering and shooting of Mobland." His eyes twinkled. "That's a dandy name you've hit on! I shall be surprised if it doesn't stick."

Carpenter went on questioning, bent upon knowing about this outlaw organization and its members. It was clear before long that he had taken a fancy to young John Colver. He made him sit beside him, and asked to hear some of his poetry, and when he found it really vivid and beautiful, he put his arm about the young poet's shoulders. Again I found memories of old childhood phrases stirring in my mind. Had there not once been a disciple named John, who was especially beloved?

XLII

PRESENTLY the young agitator began telling about an investigation he had been making in the lumber country of the Northwest. He was writing a pamphlet on the subject of a massacre which had occurred there. A mob of ex-soldiers had stormed the headquarters of the "wobblies," and the latter had defended themselves, and killed two or three of their assailants. A news agency had sent out over the country a story to the effect that the "wobblies" had made an unprovoked assault upon the ex-soldiers. "That's what the papers do to us!" said John Colver. "There have been scores of mobbings as a result, and just now it may be worth a man's life to be caught carrying a red card in any of these Western states."

So there was the subject of non-resistance, and I sat and listened with strangely mingled feelings of sympathy and repulsion, while this group of rebels of all shades and varieties argued whether it was really possible for the workers to get free without some kind of force. Carpenter, it appeared, was the only one in the company who believed it possible. The gentle Comrade Abell was obliged to admit that the Socialists, in using political action, were really resorting to force in a veiled form. They sought to take possession of the state by voting; but the state was an instrument of force, and would use force to carry out its will. "You are an anarchist!" said the Socialist lawyer, addressing Carpenter.

To my surprise Carpenter was not shocked by this.

"If I admit no power but love," said he, "how can I have anything to do with government?"

More visitors called, and were admitted, and presently the little room was packed with people, and a regular meeting was in progress. I heard more strange ideas than I had ever known existed in the world. I tried not to be offended; but I thought there ought to be at least a few words said for plain ordinary human beings who carry no labels, so I ventured now and then to put in a mild suggestion—for example, that there were quite a few people in the world who did not love all their neighbors, and could not be persuaded to love them all at once, and it might be necessary to put just a little restraint upon them for a time. Again I suggested, maybe the workers were not yet sufficiently educated to run the industries, they might need some help from the present masters. "Just a little more education," I ventured—

And John Colver laughed, the first ugly laugh I had heard from him. "Education by the masters? Education at the end of a club!"

"My boy," I argued, "I know there are plenty of employers who are rough, but there are others who are good men, who would like to change the system, would like to do something, if they knew what it was. But who will tell them what to do? Take me, for example. I have a great deal of wealth which I have not earned; but what can I do about it? What do you say, Mr. Carpenter?"

I turned to him, as the true authority; and the others also turned to him. He answered, without hesitation: "Sell everything that you have and give it to the unemployed."

"But," said I, "would that really solve the problem. They would spend it, and we should be right where we were before."

Said Carpenter: "They are unemployed because you have taken from them wealth which you have not earned. Give it back to them."

And then, seeing that I was not satisfied, he added: "How hard it is for a rich man to understand the meaning of social justice! Indeed, it would be easier for a strike leader to get the truth published in your 'Times', than for a rich man to understand what the word social justice means."

The company laughed, and I subsided, and let the wave of conversation roll by. It was only later that I realized the part I had just been playing. It had been easy for me to recognize T-S as St. Peter, but I had not known myself as that rich young man who had asked for advice, and then rejected it. "When he heard this, he was very sorrowful; for he was very rich." Yes, I had found my place in the story!

XLIII

YOU may believe that next morning my first thought was to get hold of the "Times" and see what they had done to my prophet. Sure enough, there he was on the front page, three columns wide, with the customary streamer head:

Mob Of Anarchists Raid St. Bartholmew's
Prophet And Ragged Horde Break Up Church Services

I skimmed over the story quickly; I noted that Carpenter was represented as having tried to knock down the Reverend Mr. Simpkinson, and that the prophet's followers had assaulted members of the congregation. I confess to some relief upon discovering that my own humble part in the adventure had not been mentioned. I suspected that my Uncle Timothy must have been busy at the telephone on Sunday evening! But then I turned to the "Examiner," and alas, there I was! "A certain rich young man," rising up to protect an incendiary prophet! I remembered that my Uncle Timothy had had a violent row with the publisher of the "Examiner" a year or two ago, over some political appointment!

The "Times" had another editorial, two columns, double leaded. Yesterday the paper had warned the public what to expect; today it saw the prophecies justified, and what it now wished to know was, had Western City a police department, or had it not? "How much longer do our authorities propose to give rein to this fire-brand imposter? This prophet of God who rides about town in a broken-down express-wagon, and consorts with movie actresses and red agitators! Must the police wait until his seditious doctrines have fanned the flames of mob violence beyond control? Must they wait until he has gathered all the others of his ilk, the advocates of lunacy and assassination about him, and caused an insurrection of class envy and hate? We call upon the authorities of our city to act and act at once; to put this wretched mountebank behind bars where he belongs, and keep him there."

There was another aspect of this matter upon which the "Times" laid emphasis. After long efforts on the part of the Chamber of Commerce and other civic organizations, Western City had been selected as the place for the annual convention of the Mobland Brigade. In three days this convention would be called to order, and already the delegates were pouring in by every train. What impression would they get of law and order in this community? Was this the purpose for which they had shed their blood in a dreadful war—that their country might be affronted by the ravings of an impious charlatan? What had the gold-star mothers of Western City to say to this? What did the local post of the Mobland Brigade propose to do to save the fair name of their city? Said the "Times": "If our supine authorities refuse to meet this emergency, we believe there are enough 100% Americans still among us to protect the cause of public decency, and to assert the right of Christian people to worship their God without interference from the Dictatorship of the Lunatic Asylum."

Now, I had been so much interested in Carpenter and his adventures that I had pretty well overlooked this matter of the Mobland Brigade and its convention. I belong to the Brigade myself, and ought to have been serving on the committee of arrangements; instead of which, here I was chasing around trying to save a prophet, who, it appeared, really wanted to get into trouble! Yes, the Brigade was coming; and I could foresee what would happen when a bunch of these wild men encountered Carpenter's express wagon on the street!

XLIV

I swallowed a hasty cup of coffee, and drove in a taxi to the Labor Temple. Carpenter had said he would be there early in the morning, to help with the relief work again. I went to the rooms of the Restaurant Workers, and found that he had not yet arrived. I noticed a group of half a dozen men standing near the door, and there seemed something uncordial in the look they gave me. One of them came toward me, the same who had sought my advice about permitting Carpenter to speak at the mass meeting. "Good morning," he said; and then: "I thought you told me this fellow Carpenter was not a red?"

"Well," said I, taken by surprise, "is he?"

"God Almighty!" said the other. "What do you call this?" And he held up a copy of the "Times." "Going in and shouting in the middle of a church service, and trying to knock down a clergyman!"

I could not help laughing in the man's face. "So even you labor men believe what you read in the 'Times'! It happens I was present in the church myself, and I assure you that Carpenter offered no resistance, and neither did anyone else in his group. You remember, I told you he was a man of peace, and that was all I told you."

"Well," said the other, somewhat more mildly, "even so, we can't stand for this kind of thing. That's no way to accomplish anything. A whole lot of our members are Catholics, and what will they make of carryings-on like this? We're trying to persuade people that we're a law-abiding organization, and that our officials are men of sense."

"I see," said I. "And what do you mean to do about it?"

"We have called a meeting of our executive committee this morning, and are going to adopt a resolution, making clear to the public that we knew nothing about this church raid, and that we don't stand for such things. We would never have permitted this man Carpenter to speak on our platform, if we had known about his ideas."

I had nothing to say, and I said it. The other was watching me uneasily. "We hear the man proposes to come back to our relief kitchen. Is that so?"

"I believe he does; and I suppose you would rather he didn't. Is that it?" The other admitted that was it, and I laughed. "He has had his thousand dollars worth of hospitality, I suppose."

"Well, we don't want to hurt his feelings," said the other. "Of gourse our members are having a hard time, and we were glad to get the money, but it would be better if our central organization were to contribute the funds, rather than to have us pay such a price as this newspaper publicity."

"Then let your committee vote the money, and return it to Mr. T-S, and also to Mary Magna."

It took the man sometime to figure out a reply to this proposition. "We have no objection to Mr. T-S coming here," he said, "or Miss Magna either."

"That is," said I, "so long as they obey the law, and don't get in bad with the Western City 'Times'!" After a moment I added, "You may make your mind easy. I will go downstairs and wait for Mr. Carpenter, and tell him he is not wanted."

And so I left the Labor Temple and walked up and down on the sidewalk in front. It was really rather unreasonable of me to be annoyed with this labor man for having voiced the same point of view of "common sense" which I had been defending to Carpenter's group on the previous evening. Also, I was obliged to admit to myself that if I were a labor leader, trying to hold together a group of half-educated men in the face of public sentiment such as existed in this city, I might not have the same carefree, laughing attitude towards life as a certain rich young man whose pockets were stuffed with unearned increments.

To this mood of tolerance I had brought myself, when I saw a white robe come round the corner, arm in arm with a frock coat of black broadcloth. Also there came Everett, looking still more ghastly, his nose and lip having become purple, and in places green. Also there was Korwsky, and two other men; Moneta, a young Mexican cigarmaker out of work, and a man named Hamby, who had turned up on the previous evening, introducing himself as a pacifist who had been arrested and beaten up during the war. Somehow he did not conform to my idea of a pacifist, being a solid and rather stoutish fellow, with nothing of the idealist about him. But Carpenter took him, as he took everybody, without question or suspicion.

XLV

I joined the group, and made clear to them, as tactfully as I could, that they were not wanted inside. Comrade Abell threw up his hands. "Oh, those labor skates!" he cried. "Those miserable, cowardly, grafting politicians! Thinking about nothing but keeping themselves respectable, and holding on to their fat, comfortable salaries!"

"Vell, vat you expect?" cried Korwsky. "You git de verkin' men into politics, and den you blame dem fer bein' politicians!"

"Nothing was said about returning the money, I suppose?" remarked Everett, in a bitter tone.

"Something was said," I replied. "I said it. I don't think the money will be returned."

Then Carpenter spoke. "The money was given to feed the hungry," said he. "If it is used for that purpose, we can ask no more. And if men set out to preach a new doctrine, how can they expect to be welcomed at once? We have chosen to be outcasts, and must not complain. Let us go to the jail. Perhaps that is the place for us." So the little group set out in a new direction.

On the way we talked about the labor movement, and what was the matter with it. Comrade Abell said that Carpenter was right, the fundamental trouble was that the workers were imbued with the psychology of their masters. They would strike for this or that improvement in their condition, and then go to the polls and vote for the candidates of their masters. But Korwsky was more vehement; he was an industrial unionist, and thought the present craft unions worse than nothing.

Little groups of labor aristocrats, seking to benefit themselves at the expense of the masses, the unorganized, unskilled workers and the floating population of casual labor! That was why those "skates" at the Labor Temple has so little enthusiasm for Carpenter and his doctrine of brotherhood! In this country where every man was trying to climb up on the face of some other man!

Our little group had come out on Broadway. It attracted a good deal of attention, and a number of curiosity seekers were beginning to trail behind us. "We'll get a crowd again, and Carpenter 'll be making a speech," I thought; and as usual I faced a moral conflict. Should I stand by, or should I sneak away, and preserve the dignity of my family?

Suddenly came a sound of music, fifes and drums. It burst on our ears from round the corner, shrill and lively—"The Girl I Left Behind Me." Carpenter, who was directly in front of me, stopped short, and seemed to shrink away from what was coming, until his back was against the show-window of a department-store, and he could shrink no further.

It was a company of ex-service men in uniform; one or two hundred, carrying rifles with fixed bayonets which gleamed in the sunshine. There were two fifers and two drummers at their head, and also two flags, one the flag of the Brigade, and the other the flag of Mobland. I remembered having noted in the morning papers that the national commander of the brigade was to arrive in town this morning, and no doubt this was a delegation to do him honor.

The marchers swept down on us, and past us, and I watched the prophet. His eyes were wide, his whole face expressing anguish. "Oh God, my Father!" he whispered, and seemed to quiver with each thud of the tramping feet on the pavement. After the storm had passed, he stood motionless, the pain still in his face "It is Rome! It is Rome!" he murmured.

"No," said I, "it is Mobland."

He went on, as if he had not heard me. "Rome! Eternal Rome! Rome that never dies!" And he turned upon me his startled eyes. "Even the eagles!"

For a moment I was puzzled; but then I remembered the golden eagle with wings outspread, that perches on top of our national banner. "We only use one eagle," I said, somewhat feebly.

To which he answered, "The soul of one eagle is the same as the soul of two."

Now, I had felt quite certain that Carpenter would not get along very well with the Brigade, and I was more than ever decided that he must be got out of the way somehow or other. But meantime, the first task was to get him away from this crowd which was rapidly collecting. Already he was in the full tide of a speech. "Those sharp spears! Can you not see them thrust into the bowels of human beings? Can you not see them dripping with the blood of your brothers?"

I whispered to Everett, thinking him one among this company of enthusiasts who might have a little common sense left. "We had better get him away from here!" And Everett put his hand gently on the prophet's shoulder, and said, "The prisoners in the jail are hoping for us." I took him by the other arm, and we began to lead him down the street. When we had once got him going, we walked him faster and faster, until presently the crowd was trailing out into a string of idlers and curiosity seekers, as before.

XLVI

THE party came to the city jail, and knocked for admission. But no doubt the authorities had taken consultation in the meantime, and there was no admission for prophets. The party stood on the steps, baffled and bewildered, a pitiful and pathetic little group.

For my part, I thought it just as well that Carpenter had not got inside, for I knew what he would find there. It happens that my Aunt Jennie belongs to a couple of women's clubs, and they have been making a fuss about our city jail; they have kept on making it for many years, but apparently without accomplishing anything. The place was built a generation ago, for a city of perhaps one-tenth our present size; it is old and musty, and the walls are so badly cracked that it has been condemned by the building department. It is so crowded that half a dozen men sometimes sleep on the floor of a single cell. They are devoured by vermin, and lie in semi-darkness, some of them shivering with cold and others half suffocated. They stay there, sometimes for many months unheeded, because the courts are crowded, and if Comrade Abell's word may be taken in the matter, every poor man is assumed to be guilty until he is proven innocent. I have heard Aunt Jennie arguing the matter with considerable energy. Our banks are housed in palaces, and our Chamber of Commerce and our Merchants and Manufacturers and our Real Estate Exchange and all the rest of our boosters have commodious and expensive quarters; but our prisoners lie in torment, and no one boosts for them.

Did Carpenter know these things? Had the strikers or his little company of agitators, told him about them? Suddenly he said, "Let us pray;" and there on the steps of the jail he raised his hands in invocation, and prayed for all prisoners and captives. And when he finished, Comrade Abell suddenly lifted his voice and began to sing. I would not have supposed that so big a voice could have come out of so frail a body; but I was reminded that Abell had been practicing on soap-boxes a good part of his life. He was one of these shouting evangelists—only his gospel was different. He sang:

> Arise, ye pris'ners of starvation!
> Arise, ye wretched of the earth!
> For justice thunders condemnation,
> A better world's in birth.

I think I would have shuddered, even more than I did, if I had known the name of this song; if I had realized that this group of fanatics were sounding the dread Internationale on the steps of our city jail! I suspect that what saved them was the fact that the guardians of the jail had no more idea what it was than I had!

The group had sung a couple of verses, when the iron-barred doors were opened, and a policeman stepped out. He addressed Carpenter, who was not singing. "Tell that bunch of nuts of yours to can the yowling."

To which Carpenter replied: "I tell you that if these men should hold their peace, the stones of your jail would immediately cry out!" And he turned, and looked up and down the streets of the city, and suddenly I saw that he was weeping. "Oh, Mobland, Mobland! If you had known even at this time the way of justice! But the way is hid from your eyes, and you will not see it, and now the hour is coming, the horrors of the class war are upon you, ruin and destruction are at hand! Your towers of pride shall fall, your own children shall destroy you; they shall not leave you one stone upon another, because you knew not the time for justice when it came."

The doors of the jail opened again, and three or four more policemen came out, with clubs in their hands. "Get along, now!" they said roughly, and began poking the prophet and his disciples in the back; they poked them down the stairs and along the street for a block or so—until they were sure the ears of the jail inmates would no longer be troubled by offensive sounds. But still they did not arrest them, and I marveled, wondering how long it could go on. I had an uneasy feeling that the longer the climax was postponed, the more severe it would be.

There was quite a crowd following us now, hoping that something sensational would happen. And presently a woman saw us, and rushed into the house, and came out leading a blind man, and appealing to Carpenter to restore his sight; and when he stopped to do this, there were a couple of newspaper men, and an operator with a camera, and more excitement and more crowds! So we started to walk again, and came to Main Street, which in our city is given up to ten cent picture-shows, and pawn-brokers, and old clothes shops, and eating-stands for workingmen. A block or so distant we saw a mass of people, and something warned me—my heart sank into my boots. Another mob!

XLVII

THERE was shouting, and people running from every direction. The throng would surge back, and a few run from it. "What's the matter?" I cried to one of these, and the answer was, "They're cleaning out the reds!" Comrade Abell, who knew the neighborhood, exclaimed in dismay, "It's Erman's Book Store!"

"Who's doing this?" I asked of another bystander, and the answer was, "The Brigade! They're cleaning up the city before the convention!" And Comrade Abell clasped his hands to his forehead, and wailed in despair, "It's because they've been selling the 'Liberator'! Erman told me last week he'd been warned to stop selling it!"

Now, I don't know whether or not Carpenter had ever heard of this radical monthly. But he knew that here was a mob, and people in trouble, and he shook off the hands which sought to restrain him, and pushed his way into the throng, which gave way before him, either from respect or from curiosity. I learned later that some of the mob had dragged the bookseller and his two clerks out by the rear entrance, and were beating them pretty severely. But fortunately Carpenter did not see this. All he saw were a dozen or so ex-soldiers in uniform carrying armfuls of magazines and books out into a little square, which was made by the oblique intersection of two avenues. They were dumping the stuff into a pile, and a man with a five gallon can was engaged in pouring kerosene over it.

"My friend," said Carpenter, "what is this that you do?"

The other turned upon him and stared. "What the hell you got to do with it? Get out of the way there!" And to emphasize his words he slopped a jet of kerosene over the prophet's robes.

Said Carpenter: "Do you know what a book is? One of your poets has described it as the precious life-blood of a great spirit, embalmed and preserved to all posterity."

The other laughed scornfully. "Was he talkin' about Bolsheviki books, you reckon?"

Said Carpenter: "Are you one that should be set to judge books? Have you read these that you are about to destroy?" And as the other, paying no attention, knelt down to strike a match and light the pyre, he cried, in a louder voice: "Behold what a thing is war! You have been trained to kill your fellow men; the beast has been let loose in your heart, and he raves within!"

"One of these God-damn pacifists, eh?" cried the ex-soldier; and he dropped his matches and sprang up with fists clenched. Carpenter faced him without flinching; there was something so majestic about him, the man did not strike him, he merely put his spread hand against the prophet's chest and shoved him violently. "Get back out of the way!"

I well knew the risk I was taking, but I could not refrain. "Now, look here, buddy!" I began; and the soldier whirled upon me. "You one of these Huns, too?"

"I was all through the Argonne," I said quickly. "And I belong to the Brigade."

"Oh ho! Well, pitch in here, and help carry out this bloody Arnychist literature!"

I was about to answer, but Carpenter's voice rang out again. He had turned and stretched out his arms to the crowd, and we both stopped to listen to his words.

"Shall ye be wolves, or shall ye be men? That is the choice, and ye have chosen wolfhood. The blood of your brothers is upon your hands, and murder in your hearts. You have trained your young men to be killers of their brothers, and now they know only the law of madness."

There were a dozen ex-doughboys in sound of this discourse, and I judged they would not stand much of it. Suddenly one of them began to chant; and the rest took it up, half laughing, half shouting:

> Rough! Tough!
> We're the stuff!
> We want to fight and we can't get enough!

And after that:
> Hail! Hail! The gang's all here!
> We're going to get the Kaiser!

The crowd joined in, and the words of the prophet were completely drowned out. A moment later I heard a gruff voice behind me. "Make way here!" There came a policeman, shoving through. "What's all this about?"

The fellow with the kerosene can spoke up: "Here's this damn Arnychist prophet been incitin' the crowd and preachin' sedition! You better take him along, officer, and put him somewhere he'll be safe, because me and my buddies won't stand no more Bolsheviki rantin'."

It seemed ludicrous when I looked back upon it; though at the moment I did not appreciate the funny side. Here was a group of men engaged in raiding a book-store, beating up the proprietor and his clerks, and burning a thousand dollars worth of books and magazines on the public street; but the policeman did not see a bit of that, he had no idea that any such thing was happening! All he saw was a prophet, in a white nightgown dripping with kerosene, engaged in denouncing war! He took him firmly by the arm, saying, "Come along now! I guess we've heard enough o' this;" and he started to march Carpenter down the street.

"Take me too!" cried Moneta, the Mexican, beside himself with excitement; and the policeman grabbed him with the other hand, and the three set out to march.

XLVIII

I no longer had any impulse to interfere. In truth I was glad to see the policeman, considering that his worst might be better than the mob's best. About half the crowd followed us, but the singing died away, and that gave Comrade Abell his chance. He was walking directly behind the policeman, and suddenly he raised his voice, and all the rest of the way to the station-house he provided marching tunes: first the Internationale, and then the Reg Flag, and then the Marseillaise:

> Ye sons of toil, awake to glory!
> Hark, hark! What myriads bids you rise!
> Your children, wives, and grand sires hoary—
> Behold their tears and hear their cries!

When we came to the station house, the policeman gave Moneta a shove and told him to get along; he had not done anything, and was denied the honor of being arrested. The officer pushed Carpenter through the door, and bade the rest of us keep out.

Said Abell: "I am an attorney."

"The hell you are!" said the other. "I thought you were an opery singer."

"I'm a practicing attorney," said Abell, "and I represent the man you have arrested. I presume I have a right to enter."

"And I am a prospective bondsman," I stated, with sudden inspiration. "So let me in also."

We entered, and the policeman led his prisoner to the sergeant at the desk. The latter asked the charge, and was told, "Disturbing the peace and blocking traffic."

"Now, sergeant," said I, "this is preposterous. All this prisoner did was to try to stop a mob from destroying property."

"You can tell all that to the magistrate in the morning," said the sergeant.

"What is the bail?" I demanded.

"You are prepared to put up bail?"

I answered that I was; and then for the first time Carpenter spoke. "You mean you wish to pay money to secure my release? Let there be no money paid for me."

"Let me explain, Mr. Carpenter," I pleaded. "You will accomplish nothing by spending the night in a police cell. You will have no opportunity to talk with the prisoners. They will keep you by yourself."

He answered, "My Father will be with me." And gazing into the face of the sergeant, he demanded, "Do you think you can build a cell to which my Father cannot come?"

The officer was an old hand, with a fringe of grey hair around his bald head, and no doubt he had been asked many queer questions in his day. His response was to inquire the prisoner's name; and when the prisoner kept haughty silence, he wrote down "John Doe Carpenter," and proceeded: "Where do you live?"

Said Carpenter: "The foxes have holes, and the birds of the air have nests, but he that espouses the cause of justice has no home in a world of greed."

So the sergeant wrote: "No address," and nodded to a jailer, who took the prophet by the arm and led him away through a steel-barred door.

Abell and I went outside and joined the rest of the group. None of us knew just what to do—with the exception of Everett, who sat on the steps with his notebook, and made me repeat to him word for word what Carpenter had said!

XLIX

COMRADE Abell told us where the police-court was located, and we agreed to be there at nine o'clock next morning. Then I parted from the rest, and walked until I met a taxi and drove to my rooms.

I felt desolate and forlorn. Nothing in my old life had any interest for me. This was the afternoon when I usually went to the Athletic Club to box; but now I found myself wondering, what would Carpenter say to such imitation fighting? I decided I would stay by myself for a while, and take a walk and think things over. I had been dissatisfied with my life for a long time; the glamor had begun to wear off the excitement of youth, and I had begun to suspect that my life was idle and vain. Now I knew that it was: and also I knew that the world was a place of torment and woe.

I returned late in the afternoon, and a few minutes afterwards my telephone rang, and I discovered that somebody else was dissatisfied with life.

"Hello, Billy," said the voice of T-S. "I see dat feller Carpenter is in jail. Vy don't you bail him out?"

"He won't let me," I said.

"Vell, maybe it might be a good ting to leave him in jail a veek, till dis Brigade convention gits over."

"Funny!" said I. "I had the same idea!"

"Listen," continued the other, "I been feelin' awful bad because I told dem fellers I didn't know him. D' you suppose he knows I said dat, Billy?"

"Well," said I, "he knew you were going to say it, so probably he knows you said it."

"Vell," said T-S, "maybe you laugh at me, but I been tinkin' I tell dem fellows to go to hell."

"What fellows?"

"De whole damn vorld! Billy, I like dat feller Carpenter! I never met a feller like him before. You tink he vould let me go to see him in de jail?"

"I'm sure he'd be glad to see you," I said; "if the jailers didn't object."

"Sure, I fix de jailers all right!"

"But T-S," I added, "I don't believe he'll sign any contract."

"Contract nuttin'," said T-S. "I shoost vant to see him, Billy. Is dere anyting I could do fer him?"

I thought for a moment; then I said: "You might do something for one of his friends, and that's young Everett. He got pretty badly hurt, and he's sticking at the job of taking down all Carpenter's speeches. He ought to have a surgeon, and also a first class stenographer to take turns with him. Have you got another man like him?"

"I dunno," said T-S. "You don't find a young feller like Matt Everett everyday."

I started. "What do you say is his name?"

"Matthew," said T-S. "Vy you ask?"

"Nothing," said I; "just a coincidence!"

Our conversation ended with the remark by T-S that he would call up the station-house and arrange to see Carpenter. Five minutes later the telephone rang again, and I heard the magnate's voice: "Billy, dey say he's been bailed out!"

"What?" I cried. "He declared he wouldn't have it done."

"Somebody done it vitout askin' him! De money vas paid, and dey turned him out!"

"Who did it?"

"Guess!"

"You mean it was you?"

"I vouldn't 'a dared. I only shoost found out about it. Mary Magna done it, and she's took him avay somevere."

"Good Lord!" I exclaimed; and before my mind's eye flashed another headline:

Fair Film Star Frees Love-Cult Prophet

I promised to try to find out about the prophet at once. "He won't get away," I said, "because he doesn't ride in automobiles, and he and Mary can't walk very far on the street without the newspapers finding them!"

I took my telephone-book, and looked up the name Abell. It is an unusual name, and there was only one attorney bearing it. (I was struck by the fact that the first name of this attorney was Mark.) I called him on the phone, and heard the familiar gentle voice. Yes, Comrade Carpenter had just arrived, and Miss Magna was with him. They were going to have a little party, and they would be glad to have me come. Yes, Mr. T-S would be welcome, of course. So then I called up the magnate of the pictures, and not without an inward smile, conferred on him the gracious permission to spend the evening at the headquarters of Local Western City of the Socialist Party!

L

WHEN I got to the meeting-place I found that a feast had been spread. I don't know where the money came from; maybe it was Bolshevik gold, as the enemy charged, or maybe it was the ill-gotten gains of a "million dollar movie vamp." Anyhow, there was a table spread with a couple of cloths that were clean, if ragged, and on them flowers and fruit. Carpenter was seated at the head of the table, and I noted to my surprise that he had on a beautiful robe of snow-white linen, instead of the one he had formerly worn, which was not only stained with kerosene but filthy with the dust of the streets. I learned that Mrs. T-S had brought this festal garment—a simple matter for her, because in movie studios they have wardrobe rooms where they turn out any sort of costume imaginable.

This robe was so striking that it created a little controversy. James, the carpenter, who had an ascetic spirit, considered it necessary to speak plainly, and point out that Mrs. T-S would have done better to take the money and give it to the poor. But the prophet answered: "Let this woman alone. She has done a good thing. The poor you have always with you, but me you have only for a short time. This woman has helped to make our feast happy, and men will tell about it in future years."

But that did not satisfy the ascetic James, who retired to his corner grumbling. "I know, we're going to start a new church—the same old graft all over again! A man has no business to say a thing like that. The first thing you know, they'll be taking the widow's mite to buy silk and velvet dresses for him and golden goblets for him to drink from! And then, before you know it they'll be setting him up in stained glass windows, and priests'll be wearing jewelled robes, and saying it's all right, and quoting his words!" I perceived that it wasn't so easy for a prophet to manage a bunch of disciples in these modern days!

The controversy did not seem to trouble Mrs. T-S, who was waddling about, perfectly happy in the kitchen—doing the things she would have done all the time, if her husband's social position had not required her to keep a dozen servants. Also, I noted to my great astonishment that Mary Magna, instead of taking a place at the prophet's right hand, according to the prerogative of queens, had put on a plain apron and was helping "Maw" and Mrs. Abell. More surprising yet, T-S had seated himself inconspicuously at the foot of the table, while at the prophet's right hand there sat a convict with a twenty year jail sentence hanging over him—John Colver, the "wobbly" poet! Again an ancient phrase learned in childhood came floating through my mind: "He hath put down the mighty from their seats, and exalted them of low degree!"

Somehow word had been got to all the little group of agitators of various shades. There was Korwsky, the secretary of the tailors' union—whose first name I learned was Luka; also his fellow Russian, the express-driver,—Simon Karlin, and Tom Moneta, the young Mexican cigar-maker. There was Matthew Everett, free to be a guest on this occasion, because T-S had brought along another stenographer. There was Mark Abell, and another Socialist, a young Irishman named Andy Lynch, a veteran of the late war who had come home completely cured of militarism, and was now spending his time distributing Socialist leaflets, and preaching to the workers wherever he could get two or three to listen. Also there was Hamby, the pacifist whom I did not like, and a second I. W. W., brought by Colver—a lad named Philip, who had recently been indicted by the grand jury, and was at this moment a fugitive from justice with a price upon his head.

The door of the room was opened, and another man came in; a striking figure, tall and gaunt, with old and pitifully untidy clothing, and a half month's growth of beard upon his chin. He wore an old black hat, frayed at the edges; but under this hat was a face of such gentleness and sadness that it made you think of Carpenter's own. Withal, it was a Yankee face—of that lean, stringy kind that we know so well. The newcomer's eyes fell upon Carpenter, and his face lighted; he set down an old carpet-bag that he was carrying, and stretched out his two hands, and went to him. "Carpenter! I've been looking for you!"

And Carpenter answered, "My brother!" And the two clasped hands, and I thought to myself with astonishment, "How does Carpenter know this man?"

Presently I whispered to Abell, "Who is he?" I learned that he was one I had heard of in the papers—Bartholomew Howard, the "millionaire hobo;" he was grandson and heir of one of our great captains of industry, and had taken literally the advice of the prophet, to sell all that he had and give it to the unemployed. He traveled over the country, living among the hobos and organizing them into his Brotherhood. Now you would have thought that he and Carpenter had known each other all their lives; as I watched them, I found myself thinking: "Where are the clergy and the pillars of St. Bartholomew's Church?" There were none of them at this supper-party!

LI

T-S had stopped at a caterer's on his way to the gathering, and had done his humble best in the form of a strawberry short-cake almost half as large around as himself; also several bottles of purple color, with the label of grape juice. When the company gathered at the table and these bottles were opened, they made a suspicious noise, and so we all made jokes, as people have the habit of doing in these days of getting used to prohibition. I noticed that Carpenter laughed at the jokes, and seemed to enjoy the whole festivity.

It happened that fate had placed me next to James, so I listened to more asceticism. "He oughtn't to do things like this! People will say he likes to eat rich food and to drink. It's bad for the movement for such things to be said."

"Cheer up, my friend!" I laughed. "Even the Bolsheviks have a feast now and then, when they can get it."

"You'll see what the newspapers do with this tomorrow," growled the other; "then you won't think it so funny."

"Forget it!" I said. "There aren't any reporters here."

"No," said he, "but there are spies here, you may be sure. There are spies everywhere, nowadays. You'll see!"

Presently Carpenter called on some of the company for speeches. Would Bartholomew tell about the unemployed, what their organization was doing, and what were their plans? And after that he asked John Colver, who sat on his right hand, to recite some of his verses. John and his friend Philip, a blue eyed, freckle-faced lad who looked as if he might be in high school, told stories about the adventures of outlaw agitators. For several months these two had been traveling the country as "blanket stiffs," securing employment in lumber-camps and mines, gathering the workers secretly in the woods to listen to the new gospel of deliverance. The employers were organized on a nation-wide scale everywhere throughout the country, and the workers with their feeble craft unions were like men using bows and arrows against machine-guns. There must be One Big Union— that was the slogan, and if you preached it, you went every hour in peril of such a fate that you counted fourteen years in jail as comparatively a happy ending.

Said Carpenter: "It is not such a bad thing for a cause to have its preachers go to jail."

"Well," said the lad of the blue eyes and the freckled face, "we try to keep a few outside, to tell what the rest are in for!"

Later on, I remember, John Colver told a funny story about this pal of his. The story had to do with grape juice instead of with propaganda, but it appealed to me because it showed the gay spirit of these lads. The two of them had sought refuge from a storm in a barn, and there, lying buried in the hay with the rain pouring down on the roof, they had heard the farmer coming to milk his cows. The man had evidently just parted from his wife, and there had been a quarrel; but the farmer hadn't dared to say what he wanted to, so now he took it out on the cows! "Na! na! na!" he shouted, with furious vehemence. "That's it!

Go on! Nag, nag, nag! Don't stop, or I might manage to get a word in! Yes, I'm late, of course I'm late Do you expect me to drive by the clock? Maybe I did forget the sugar! Maybe I've got nothing on my mind but errands! Whiskey? Maybe it's whiskey, and maybe it's gin, and maybe it's grape-juice!" The farmer set down his milk-pail and his lantern, and shook his clenched fist at the patient cattle. "I'm a man, I am, and I'll have you understand I'm master in my own house! I'll drink if I feel like drinking, I'll stop and chat with my neighbors if I feel like stopping, I'll buy sugar if I remember to buy it, and if you don't like it, you can buy your own!" And so on—becoming more inspired with his own eloquence—or maybe with the whiskey, or the gin, or the grape-juice; until young Philip became so filled with the spirit of the combat that he popped up out of the hay and shouted, "Good for you, old man! Stand up for your rights! Don't let her down you! Hurrah for men!" And the astounded farmer stood staring with his mouth open, while the two "wobbles" leaped up and fled from the barn, so convulsed with laughter they hardly noticed the floods of rain pouring down upon them.

LII

BUT, of course, it wasn't long before this little company became serious again. Carpenter told Franklin that he ought not stay here; he, Carpenter, was too conspicuous a figure, the authorities were certain to be watching him. Korwsky backed him up. There were sure to be spies here! They would never leave such a man unwatched. They would set to work to get something on him, and if they couldn't get it they would make it. When Carpenter asked what he meant, he explained, "Dey'll plant dynamite in de place vere you are, or dey'll fake up some letters to show you been plannin' violence."

"And do people believe such things?" asked Carpenter.

"Believe dem?" cried Korwsky. "If dey see it in de papers, dey believe it—sure dey do!"

The prophet answered, "Let a man live so that the world will believe him and not his enemies." Then he added a startling remark. "There is one among us who will betray me."

Of course, they all looked at one another in consternation. They were deeply distressed, and each tried in turn—"Comrade," or "Brother," or "Fellow-worker," or whatever term they used—"is it I?" Presently the sturdy looking fellow named Hamby, who called himself a pacifist, asked, "Is it I?" And Carpenter answered, quietly, "You have said it."

Then, of course, some of the others started up; they wanted to throw him out, but Carpenter bade them sit down again, saying, "Let things take their course; for the powers of this world will perish more quickly if they are permitted to kill themselves."

Apparently he saw no reason why this episode should be permitted to interfere with the festivities. Mary Magna came in laughing, bearing the strawberry short-cake, and set it on the table and proceeded to portion it out. When it was served, Carpenter said, "I shall not be with you much longer, my friends; but you will remember me when you see this beautiful red fruit on top of a cake; and also you will think of me and my message when you taste rich purple grape-juice that has perhaps stayed a day or two too long in the bottle!"

Some of the company laughed, but others of them had tears in their eyes; and I noticed that in the midst of the merriment the fellow Hamby got up and slipped out of the room. Not long after that the company began to disperse for various reasons. Karlin explained that his old horse had been working all day, and had had no supper. Colver was uneasy, not for himself, but for his friend, and I saw him start every time the door was opened. Also, T-S was having some night-scenes taken, and he and Mary were to see the work. Finally Carpenter dismissed the Company, with the statement that he wished to retire to Comrade Abell's private office to pray; and Abell and his friend Lynch and the young Mexican said they would watch and wait for him. The rest of us took our departure, not without misgivings and sorrow in our hearts.

LIII

NOW, you may find it hard to believe a confession which I have put off making—the fact that at this time I was engaged to be married. There was a certain member of what is called the "younger set," whom I had given reason to expect that I would think about her at least once in a while. But here for precisely three days I had been chasing about at the skirts of a prophet fresh from God, getting my name into the newspapers in scandalous fashion, and not daring even to call the young lady on the telephone and make apologies. That evening there was a dinner-dance at her home, and I supposed I was supposed to be there; but no one had bothered to invite me, and as a matter of fact I would not have known of the affair if I had not seen the announcement in the papers. I was too late for the dinner, but I got myself a taxicab, and drove to my room and changed my clothes, and hurried in my own car to the dance.

You would not be interested in the fact that when I arrived I was treated as an unwelcome guest, and Miss Betty even went so far as to remind me that I had not been invited. But after I had pleaded, she consented to dance with me; and so for an hour or two I tried to forget there were any people in the world who had anything to do but be happy. Just as I was succeeding, the butler came, calling me to the telephone, and I answered, and who should it be but Old Joe!

My surprise became consternation at his first words: "Billy, your friend Carpenter is in peril!"

"What do you mean?"

"They are going to get him tonight."

"Good God! How do you know?"

"It's a long story, and no time to tell it. Somebody's tipped me off. Where can I meet you? Every minute is precious."

"Where are you?" I asked, and learned that he was at his home, not far away. I said I would come there, and I hurried to Betty and had another scene with her, and left her weeping, vowing that she would never see me again. I ran out and jumped into my car—and I would hate to tell what I did to the speed laws of Western City. Suffice it to say that a few minutes later I was in Old Joe's den, and he was telling me his story.

Part of it I got then, and part of it later, but I might as well tell it all at once and be done with it. It happened that at the restaurant where Old Joe and I had dined before we went to the mass-meeting, he had met a girl whom he knew too well, after the fashion of young men about town. In greeting her on the way out, he had told her he was going to hear the new prophet and had laughingly suggested that the meeting was free. The girl, out of idle curiosity, had come, and had been touched by Carpenter's physical, if not by his moral charms. It chanced that this girl was living with a man who stood high in the secret service department of "big business" in our city; so she had got the full story of what was being planned against Carpenter. That afternoon, it appeared, there had been a meeting between Algernon de Wiggs, president of our Chamber of Commerce, and Westerly, secretary of our "M. and M.," and Gerald Carson, organizer of our "Boosters' League." These three had put up six thousand dollars, and turned it over to their secret service agents, with instructions that Carpenter's agitations in Western City were to be ended inside of twenty-four hours.

A plan had been worked out, every detail of which had been phoned to Old Joe. A group of ex-service men, members of the Brigade, had been hired to seize the prophet and treat him to a tar and feathering. It had not taken much to move them to action, for the afternoon papers were full of accounts of Carpenter's speech on Main Street, his denunciation of war, and of soldiers as "murderers" and "wolves."

But that was not all, said Old Joe; and I saw that his hand was trembling as he spoke. It appeared that there was an "operative" named Hamby, who was one of Carpenter's followers.

"By God!" I burst out, in sudden fury. "I was sure that fellow was a crook!"

"Yes," said the other. "He's been telephoning in regular reports as to Carpenter's doings. And now it's been arranged that he is to put an infernal machine in the Socialist headquarters where Carpenter has been staying!"

I was almost speechless. "You mean—to blow them up?"

"No, to blow up their reputations. Hamby is to lure Carpenter out to the street, and when the gang grabs him, Hamby will fire a shot, and there will be three or four secret agents in the crowd, who will incite the others, and see to it that Carpenter is lynched instead of being tarred and feathered!"

LIV

SO there was the layout; and now, what was to be done? The first thing was to call Abell on the phone, and see if anything had happened. I picked up the receiver; but alas, the report was, "No answer." I urged "central" to try several times, but all I could get was, "I am ringing them." Carpenter, no doubt, was praying. What were the others doing? I kept on trying, but finally gave up.

Could the mob have taken them away? But Old Joe answered, no, a definite hour had been set. The ex-service men were to gather on the stroke of midnight. We had nearly an hour yet.

My first thought was that we should hurry to the Socialist headquarters and get Carpenter out of the way. But my friend pointed out that the place was certain to be watched, and we might find ourselves held up by the armed detectives; they would hardly take a chance of letting their prey escape at this hour. Also, I realized there was no use figuring on any plan that involved spiriting Carpenter away quietly, by the roof, or a rear entrance, or anything of that sort. He would insist on staying and facing his enemies.

I put my wits to work. We needed a good-sized crowd; we needed, in fact, a mob of our own. And suddenly the word brought to me an inspiration; that mob which T-S had drilled at Eternal City! I recalled that a year or so ago I had been lured to sit through a very dull feature picture which the magnate had made, showing the salvation of our country by the Ku Klux Klan; and I knew enough about studio methods to be sure they had not thrown away the costumes, but would have them stored. Here was the way to save our prophet! Here was the way to get what one wanted in Mobland!

I picked up the receiver and called Eternal City. Yes, Mr. T-S was there, but he was "on the lot" and could not be disturbed. I gave my name, and stated that it was a matter of life and death; Mr. T-S must come to the phone instantly. A couple of minutes later I heard his voice, and told him the situation, and also my scheme. He must come himself, to make sure that his orders were obeyed; he must bring several bus-loads of men, clad in the full regalia of Mobland's great Secret Society; and they must arrive at Abell's place precisely on the stroke of midnight. The men must be paid five dollars apiece, and be told that if they succeeded in bringing away the prophet unharmed, they would each get ten dollars extra. "I will put up that money," I said to T-S; but to my surprise he cried: "You ain't gonna put up nuttin'! God damn dem fellers, I'll beat 'em if it costs me a million!" So I realized that the prophet had made one more convert!

"Have you got that bus with the siren?" I asked; and when he answered, yes, I said, "Let that be the signal. When we hear it, Joe and I will bring Carpenter down to the street, and if the Brigade is there, it's up to you to persuade them you're the bigger mob!"

Then Old Joe and I ran down to my car, and drove at full speed to the Socialist headquarters; and on the way we worked out our own plan of campaign. The real danger-point was Hamby, the secret agent, and we must manage to put him out of the way. Despite his pose of "pacifism," he was certain to be armed, said Old Joe; yet we must take a chance, and do the job unarmed. If we should get into a shooting-scrape, they would certainly put it onto us; and they would make it a hanging matter, too.

I named over the members of Carpenter's party who had stayed with him. Andy Lynch, the ex-soldier, was probably a useful man, and we would get his help. We would get rid of Hamby, and then we would wait for T-S and his siren. By the time these plans were thoroughly talked out, we had reached the building in which the headquarters were located. There were lights in the main room upstairs, and the door which led up to them was open. The street was apparently deserted, and we did not stop to look for any "operatives," but left our machine and stole quietly upstairs and into the room.

LV

COMRADE Abell sat at the table, with his head bowed in his arms, sound asleep. Lynch, the ex-soldier, and Tom Moneta, the Mexican, were lying on the floor snoring. And on a chair near the doorway, watching the scene, sat Hamby, wide awake. We knew he was awake, because he leaped to his feet the instant we entered the door. "Oh, it's you!" he said, recognizing me; I noted the alarm in his voice.

I beckoned to him, softly. "Come here a moment;" and he came out into the ante-room. At the same time Old Joe stepped across the big room, and stooped down and waked up Lynch. We had agreed that Joe was to give Lynch a whispered explanation of the situation, while I kept Hamby busy.

"Where is Mr. Carpenter?" I asked.

"He's in the private office, praying."

"Well," said I, "there's a sick woman who needs help very badly. I wonder if we'd better disturb him."

"I don't know," said Hamby. "I've been here an hour, and haven't heard a sound. Maybe he's asleep."

I was uncertain what I should do, and I elaborately explained my uncertainty. Of course, praying was an important and useful occupation, and I knew that the prophet laid great stress upon it, and all of us who loved him so dearly must respect his wishes.

"Yes, of course," said Hamby.

Yet at the same time, I continued, this woman was very ill, a case of ptomaine poisoning—

"Do you think he can cure that?" asked Hamby guilelessly; and at that moment Old Joe and Lynch came from the big room. Hamby started to turn, but he was too late. Old Joe's arms went around him, and Hamby's two elbows were clamped to his sides, in a grip which more than one professional wrestler in our part of the world has found it impossible to break. At the same time I stooped on my knees and grasped the man's two wrists; because we were taking no chances of his gun. Lynch, the ex-soldier, had a cloth, taken from the big table, and he flung this over the head of the "pacifist" and stifled his cries.

I took a revolver from his hip-pocket, but Joe was not satisfied. "Search him carefully," said he, and so I discovered another weapon in a side-pocket. Then I made hasty search in a big closet of the room, and found a lot of bundles of books and magazines tied with stout cords. I took the cords, and we bound the "pacifist's" wrists and ankles, and put a gag in his mouth, and then we felt sure he was really a pacifist. We carried him to the closet and laid him on the floor, where a humorous idea came to us. These bundles of magazines and books were no doubt the ones which the mob had confiscated from Comrade Abell. Since they were no longer saleable, they might as well be put to some use, so I gathered armfuls of them and distributed them over the form of Hamby, until there was no longer a trace of him visible.

And while I was doing this, I noticed in one corner of the closet, under the bundles, a wooden box about a foot square. Upon trying to lift it, I discovered that it weighed several times as much as it should have weighed if it had contained printed matter. "Here's our infernal machine," I whispered, and I picked it up gingerly, and tiptoed out of the room, and back to the kitchen, and down a rear stairway of the building. I unlocked the door and opened it—and there, crouching in the shadows alongside the door, just as I expected, I saw a man.

"Hello!" I whispered.

"Hello!" said he, badly startled.

"Here's something belonging to Hamby. He wants me to give it to you. Be careful, it's heavy." I deposited the box in his hands, and shut the door, and turned the lock again, and groped my way upstairs, chuckling to myself as I imagined the man's plight. He would not know what to make of this incident, and I had an idea he would not be able to find out, because he could not leave his post. Nor would he have much time to figure over the matter; for when I got back to the light, I looked at my watch, and it lacked just three minutes to twelve.

I found that Lynch and Old Joe had shut the pacifist in the closet, and were in the ante-room waiting for me. I whispered that everything was all right. A moment later we heard a sound in the big room, and peered in, and saw a door at the far end open—and there was Carpenter, standing with his white robes gleaming in the light. After a moment I realized that they gleamed even more than was natural; I perceived once more that strange "aura" which had been noticed at the mass-meeting; and by means of it I noticed an even more startling thing. There were drops of sweat on Carpenter's forehead, as always when he had labored intensely in his soul. This time I saw that the drops were large, and they were drops of blood!

A trembling seized me. I was awe-stricken before this man—afraid to go on with what I was doing, and equally afraid to back out. I remained staring helplessly, and saw him approach the sleeping figures, and stand looking at them. "Could you not watch with me one hour?" he said, in his gentle, sad voice; and he put his hand on Comrade Abell's shoulder, with the words: "The time has come."

Abell started to his feet, and began to apologize. The other said nothing, but stooped and waked Moneta. And at that moment I heard the shrill blast of a whistle outside on the street! "There's the Brigade!" whispered Old Joe.

LVI

I ran down the stairs, and peered through the doorway, and sure enough, there were four or five automobiles stopped before the headquarters, having approached from opposite direction. I stood just long enough to see a crowd of men in khaki uniforms jumping out; then I ran back, and leaving Old Joe and Lynch to keep guard at the top of the stairs, I walked in and greeted Carpenter.

He expressed no surprise at seeing me. Evidently his thoughts were on other things. For my part, I was trembling with excitement, so that my knees would barely hold me. How long would it be before T-S and his crowd appeared? I could figure the time it should take them to drive from Eternal City; but suppose something held them up? How long would the ex-service men stay out on the street, waiting for Hamby to answer their signal? Surely not many minutes! They would storm the place, and hunt out their victim for themselves. And suppose they should carry him off before the others arrived?

I had Hamby's two revolvers in my pocket. Should we use them, or not? The thought hit me all of a sudden; and apparently it hit Old Joe at the same moment. "Give me those guns, Billy," he whispered, and I put them obediently into his hands, and he went quickly into the rear rooms. At the end of a minute, he returned, saying, "I unloaded them and threw them out of the back window." And even as he spoke, the silence of the night outside was shattered by the scream of that siren, which served to warn people out of the way when T-S was moving his companies about "on location."

I went up to Carpenter. I didn't enjoy telling him a lie; in fact, I had an idea that one couldn't lie to him successfully. But I tried it. "Mr. Carpenter, Hamby left a message; he had to go downstairs, and said he wanted to see you. Would you come down and meet him?"

"Ah, yes!" said Carpenter. And he walked to the door and down the stairs without another word. The rest of us followed him; Abell and Moneta first, they being innocent and unsuspicious; and then Lynch, and then Joe and I.

The prophet stepped out to the street, and was instantly surrounded by a group of a dozen ex-service men, two of whom grasped him by the arms. He did not lift a hand, nor even make a sound. Comrade Abell, of course, started to cry out in protest; Moneta, the Mexican, reverted to his ancestors. His hand flashed to an inside pocket, and a knife leaped out. A soldier had hold of him, and Moneta shouted, "Stand back, or I cut off your ears." At which Carpenter turned, and in a stern, commanding voice proclaimed: "Let no man use force in my behalf! They who use force shall perish by force." Moneta stood still; and of course Lynch and Old Joe and I stood still; and the dozen men about Carpenter started to lead him away to their automobiles.

But they did not get very far. Upon the silence of the street a voice rang out. Ordinarily, one would have known it was the voice of a woman; but in this place, under these exciting circumstances, it seemed the voice of a supernatural being. It almost sang the words; it was like a silver bugle calling across a battle-field—glorious, thrilling, hypnotic. "Make way-y-y-y for the Grand Imperial Klee-e-agle of the Ku-u Klux Klan!" Every one was startled; but I think I was startled more that the rest, for I knew the voice! Mary Magna had taken another speaking part!

I was on the steps of the building, so I could see over the heads of the crowd. There were four of the big busses from Eternal City, two having approached from each direction. Some fifty figures had descended from them, and others were still descending, each one clad in a voluminous white robe, with a white hood over the head, and two black holes for eyes, and another for the nose. These figures had spread out in a half moon, entirely surrounding the little mob of ex-service men, and penning them against the wall of the building. In the center of the half moon, standing a few feet in advance, was the figure of the "Grand Imperial Kleagle," with a red star upon the forehead of the white hood, and shrouded white arms stretched out, and in one hand a magic wand with a red light on the end. This wand was waving over the Brigade members, and had apparently its full supernatural effect, for one and all they stood rooted to the spot, staring with wide-open eyes.

LVII

THE grand-opera voice raised again its silver chant: "Give way, all mobs! Yield! Retire! Abdicate!—Bow down-n-n-n! Make way for the Mob of Mobs, the irresistible, imperial, superior super-mob! Hearken to the Lord High Chief Commanding Dragon of the Esoteric Cohorts, the Exalted Immortal Grand Imperial Kleagle of the Ku Klux Klan!"

Then the Grand Imperial Kleagle turned and addressed the white-robed throng in a voice of sharp command: "Klansmen! Remember your oath! The hour of Judgment is here! The guilty wretch cowers! The grand insuperable sentence has been spoken! Coelum animum imperiabilis senescat! Similia similibus per quantum imperator. Inexorabilis ingenium parasimilibua esperantur! Saeva itnparatus ignotum indignatio! Salvo! Suppositio! Indurato! Klansmen, kneel!"

As one man, the host fell upon its knees.

"Klansmen, swear! Si fractus illibatur orbis, impavidum ferient ruinae! You have heard the sentence. What is the penalty? Is it death?"

And a voice in the crowd cried "Death!" And the others took it up; there was a roar: "Death! Death!"

Said the Grand Imperial Kleagle: "Arma virumque cano, tou poluphlesboiou thalasses!" Then, facing the staring ex-servicemen: "Tetlathi mater erne kai anaskeo ko-omeneper!"

Finally the Grand Imperial Kleagle pointed her shrouded white arm at Carpenter, who stood, as pale as death, but unflinchingly. "Death to all traitors!" she cried. "Death to all agitators! Death to all enemies of the Ku Klux Klan! Condemnatus! Incomparabilis! Ingenientis exequatur! Let the Loyal High Inexorable Guardians and the Grand Holy Seneschals of the Klan advance!"

Six shrouded figures stepped out from the crowd. Said the Grand Imperial Kleagle: "Possess yourselves of the body of this guilty wretch!" And to the ex-servicemen: "Yield up this varlet to the High Secret Court-martial of the Klan, which alone has power to punish such as he."

What the bewildered members of the Brigade made of all this hocus-pocus I had no idea. Afterwards, when the adventure was over, I asked Mary, "Where in the world did you get that stuff?" And she told me how she had once acted in a children's comedy, in which there was an old magician who spent his time putting spells on people. She had had to witness his incantations eight or ten times a week for nearly a year, so of course the phrases had got fixed in her memory, and they had served just as well to impress these grown-up children.

Or perhaps the ex-servicemen thought this might be a further plan of those who had employed them. Whatever they thought, it was obvious that they were hopelessly outnumbered. There could be nothing for a mob to do but yield to a Super-mob; and they yielded. Those who were in front of Carpenter stepped back, and the Loyal High Inexorable Guardians and the Grand Holy Seneschals took Carpenter by the arms and led him away. Apparently they were going to overlook the rest of us; but Old Joe and Lynch and myself took Abell and

Moneta by the shoulders and shoved them along, past the ex-service men and into the midst of the "Klansmen."

There was no need to consider dignity after that. We hustled Carpenter to the nearest of the busses, and put him in; the Grand Imperial Kleagle followed, and the rest of us clambered in after her. Sitting up beside the driver, watching the scene, was T-S, beaming with delight; he got me by the hand and wrung it. I could not speak, my teeth were literally chattering with excitement. Carpenter, sitting in the seat behind us, must have realized by now the meaning of this scandalous adventure; but he said not a word, and the white-gowned Klansmen piled in behind him, and the siren shrieked out into the night, and the bus backed to the corner, and turned and sped off; and all the way to Eternal City, T-S and I and Old Joe slapped one another on the back and roared with laughter, and the rest of the Klansmen roared with laughter—all save the Grand Imperial Kleagle, who sat by Carpenter's side, and was discovered to be weeping.

LVIII

T-S and I had exchanged a few whispered words, and decided that we would take Carpenter to his place, which was a few miles in the country from Eternal City. He would be as safe there as anywhere I could think of. When we had got to the studios, we discharged our Klansmen, and arranged to send Old Joe to his home, and the three disciples to a hotel for the night; then I invited Carpenter to step into T-S's car. He had not spoken a word, and all he said now was, "I wish to be alone."

I answered: "I am taking you to a place where you may be alone as long as you choose." So he entered the car, and a few minutes later T-S and I were escorting him into the latter's showy mansion.

We were getting to be rather scared now, for Carpenter's silence was forbidding. But again he said: "I wish to be alone." We took him upstairs to a bed-room, and shut him in and left him—but taking the precaution to lock the door.

Downstairs, we stood and looked at each other, feeling like two school-boys who had been playing truant, and would soon have to face the teacher. "You stay here, Billy!" insisted the magnate. "You gotta see him in de mornin'! I von't!"

"I'll stay," I said, and looked at my watch. It was after one o'clock. "Give me an alarm-clock," I said, "because Carpenter wakes with the birds, and we don't want him escaping by the window."

So it came about that at daybreak I tapped on Carpenter's door, softly, so as not to waken him if he were asleep. But he answered, "Come in;" and I entered, and found him sitting by the window, watching the dawn.

I stood timidly in the middle of the room, and began: "I realize, of course, Mr. Carpenter, that I have taken a very great liberty with you—"

"You have said it," he replied; and his eyes were awful.

"But," I persisted, "if you knew what danger you were in—"

Said he: "Do you think that I came to Mobland to look for a comfortable life?"

"But," I pleaded, "if you only knew that particular gang! Do you realize that they had planted an infernal machine, a dynamite bomb, in that room? And all the world was to read in the newspapers this morning that you had been conspiring to blow up somebody!"

Said Carpenter: "Would it have been the first time that I have been lied about?"

"Of course," I argued, "I know what I have done—"

"You can have no idea what you have done. You are too ignorant."

I bowed my head, prepared to take my punishment. But at once Carpenter's voice softened. "You are a part of Mobland," he said; "you cannot help yourself. In Mobland it is not possible for even a martyrdom to proceed in an orderly way."

I gazed at him a moment, bewildered. "What's the good of a martyrdom?" I cried.

"The good is, that men can be moved in no other way; they are in that childish stage of being, where they require blood sacrifice."

"But what kind of martyrdom!" I argued. "So undignified and unimpressive! To have hot tar smeared over your body, and be hanged by the neck like a common criminal!"

I realized that this last phrase was unfortunate. Said Carpenter: "I am used to being treated as a common criminal."

"Well," said I, in a voice of despair, "of course, if you're absolutely bent on being hanged—if you can't think of anything you would prefer—"

I stopped, for I saw that he had covered his face with his hands. In the silence I heard him whisper: "I prayed last night that this cup might pass from me; and apparently my prayer has been answered."

"Well," I said, deciding to cheer up, "you see, I have only been playing the part of Providence. Let me play it just a few days longer, until this mob of crazy soldier-boys has got out of town again. I am truly ashamed for them, but I am one of them myself, so I understand them. They really fought and won a war, you see, and they are full of the madness of it, the blind, intense passions—"

Carpenter was on his feet. "I know!" he exclaimed. "I know! You need not tell me about that! I do not blame your soldier-boys. I blame the men who incite them—the old men, the soft-handed men, who sit back in office-chairs and plan madness for the world! What shall be the punishment of these men?"

"They're a hard crowd—" I admitted.

"I have seen them! They are stone-faced men! They are wolves with machinery! They are savages with polished fingernails! And they have made of the land a place of fools! They have made it Mobland!"

I did not try to answer him, but waited until the storm of his emotion passed. "You are right, Mr. Carpenter. But that is the fact about our world, and you cannot change it—"

Carpenter flung out his arm at me. "Let no man utter in my presence the supreme blasphemy against life!"

So, of course, I was silent; and Carpenter went and sat at the window again, and watched the dawn.

At last I ventured: "All that your friends ask, Mr. Carpenter, is that you will wait until this convention of the ex-soldiers has got out of town. After that, it may be possible to get people to listen to you. But while the Brigade is here, it is impossible. They are rough, and they are wild; they are taking possession of the city, and will do what they please. If they see you on the streets, they will inflict indignities upon you, they will mishandle you—"

Said Carpenter: "Do not fear those who kill the body, but fear those who kill the soul."

So again I fell silent; and presently he remarked: "My brother, I wish to be alone."

Said I: "Won't you please promise, Mr. Carpenter—"

He answered: "I make promises only to my Father. Let me be."

LIX

I went downstairs, and there was T-S, wandering around like a big fat monk in a purple dressing gown. And there was Maw, also—only her dressing gown was rose-pink, with white chrysanthemums on it. It took a lot to get those two awake at six o'clock in the morning, you may be sure; but there they were, very much worried. "Vot does he say?" cried the magnate.

"He won't say what he is going to do."

"He von't promise to stay?"

"He won't promise anything."

"Veil, did you lock de door?"

I answered that I had, and then Maw put in, in a hurry: "Billy, you gotta stay here and take care of him! If he vas to gome downstairs and tell me to do someting, I vould got to do it!"

I promised; and a little later they got ready a cup of coffee and a glass of milk and some rolls and butter and fruit, and I had the job of taking up the tray and setting it in the prophet's room. When I came in, I tried to say cheerfully, "Here's your breakfast," and not to show any trace of my uneasiness.

Carpenter looked at me, and said: "You had the door locked?"

I summoned my nerve, and answered, "Yes."

Said he: "What is the difference to me between being your prisoner and being the prisoner of your rulers?"

Said I: "Mr. Carpenter, the difference is that we don't intend to hang you."

"And how long do you propose to keep me here?"

"For about four days," I said; "until the convention disbands. If you will only give me your word to wait that time, you may have the freedom of this beautiful place, and when the period is over, I pledge you every help I can give to make known your message to the people."

I waited for an answer, but none came, so I set down the tray and went out, locking the door again. And downstairs was one of T-S's secretaries, with copies of the morning newspapers, and I picked up a "Times," and there was a headline, all the way across the page:

KU KLUX KLAN KIDNAPS KARPENTER RANTING RED PROPHET DISAPPEARS IN TOOTING AUTOS

I understood, of icourse, that the secret agency which had engineered the mobbing of the prophet would have had their stories all ready for our morning newspapers—stories which played up to the full the finding of an infernal machine, and an unprovoked attack upon ex-service men by the armed followers of the "Red Prophet." But now all this was gone, and instead was a story glorifying the Klansmen as the saviors of the city's good name. It was evident that up to the hour of going to press, neither of the two newspapers had any idea but that the white robed figures were genuine followers of the "Grand Imperial Kleagle." The "Times" carried at the top of its editorial page a brief comment in large type, congratulating the people of Western City upon the promptness with which they had demonstrated their devotion to the cause of law and order.

But of course the truth about our made-to-order mob could not be kept very long. When you have hired a hundred moving-picture actors to share in the greatest mystery of the age, it will not be many hours before your secret has got to the newspaper offices. As a matter of fact, it wasn't two hours before the "Evening Blare" was calling the home of the movie magnate to inquire where he had taken the kidnapped prophet; there was no use trying to deny anything, said the editor, diplomatically, because too many people had seen the prophet transferred to Mr. T-S's automobile. Of course T-S's secretary, who answered the phone, lied valiantly; but here again, we knew the truth would leak. There were servants and chauffeurs and gardeners, and all of them knew that the white robed mystery was somewhere on the place. They would be offered endless bribes—and some of them would accept!

In the course of the next hour or two there were a dozen newspaper reporters besieging the mansion, and camera men taking pictures of it, and even spying with opera glasses from a distance. Before my mind's eye flashed new headlines:

Movie Magnate Hides Mob Prophet From Law

This was an aspect of the matter which we had at first overlooked. Carpenter was due at Judge Ponty's police-court at nine o'clock that morning. Was he going? demanded the reporters, and if not, why not? Mary Magna no doubt would be willing to sacrifice the two hundred dollars bail that she had put up; but the judge had a right to issue a bench warrant and send a deputy for the prisoner. Would he do it?

Behind the scenes of Western City's government there began forthwith a tremendous diplomatic duel. Who it was that wanted Carpenter dragged out of his hiding-place, we could not be sure, but we knew who it was that wanted him to stay hidden! I called up my uncle Timothy, and explained the situation. It wasn't worth while for him to waste his breath scolding, I was going to stand by my prophet. If he wanted to put an end to the scandal, let him do what he could to see that the prophet was let alone.

"But, Billy, what can I do?" he cried. "It's a matter of the law."

I answered: "Fudge! You know perfectly well there's no magistrate or judge in this city that won't do what he's told, if the right people tell him. What I want you to do is to get busy with de Wiggs and Westerly and Carson, and the rest of the big gang, and persuade them that there's nothing to be gained by dragging Carpenter out of his hiding-place."

What did they want anyway? I argued. They wanted the agitation stopped. Well, we had stopped it, and without any bloodshed. If they dragged the prophet out from concealment, and into a police court, they would only have more excitement, more tumult, ending nobody could tell how.

I called up several other people who might have influence; and meanwhile T-S was over at his office in Eternal City, pleading over the telephone with the editors of afternoon papers. They had got the Red Prophet out of the way during the convention, and why couldn't they let well enough alone? Wasn't there news enough, with five or ten thousand war-heroes coming to town, without bothering about one poor religious freak?

When you shoot a load of shot at a duck, and the bird comes tumbling down, you do not bother to ask which particular shot it was that hit the target. And so it was with these frantic efforts of ours. One shot must have hit, for at eleven o'clock that morning, when the case of John Doe Carpenter versus the Commonwealth of Western City was reached in Judge Ponty's court, and the bailiff called the name of the defendant and there was no answer, the magistrate in a single sentence declared the bail forfeited, and passed on to the next case without a word. And all three of our afternoon newspapers reported this incident in an obscure corner on an inside page. The Red Prophet was dead and buried!

LX

I took up Carpenter's lunch at one o'clock, and discovered, to my dismay, that he had not tasted his breakfast. I ventured to speak to him; but he sat on a chair, gazing ahead of him and paying no attention to me, so I left him alone. At six o'clock in the evening I took up his dinner, and discovered that he had not touched either breakfast or lunch; but still he had nothing to say, so I took back the dinner, and went downstairs, and said to T-S: "We've got ourselves in for a hunger strike!"

Needless to say, under the circumstances we did not very heartily enjoy our own dinner. And T-S, neglecting his important business, stayed around; getting up out of one chair and walking nowhere, and then sitting down in another chair. I did the same, and after we had exchanged chairs a dozen times—it being then about eight o'clock in the evening—I said: "By the way, hadn't you better call up the morning papers and persuade them to be decent." So T-S seated himself at the telephone, and asked for the managing editor of the Western City "Times," and I sat and listened to the conversation.

It began with a reminder of the amount of advertising space which Eternal City consumed in the "Times" in the course of a year, and also the amount of its payroll in the community. It wasn't often that T-S asked favors, but he wanted to ask one now; he wanted the "Times" to let up on this prophet business, and especially about the prophet's connection with the moving picture industry. Everything was quiet now, the prophet wasn't bothering anybody—

Suddenly, at the height of his eloquence, T-S stopped; and it seemed to me as if he jumped a foot out of his chair. "VOT!" And then, "Vy man, you're crazy!" He turned upon me, his eyes wide with dismay. "Billy! Dey got a report—Carpenter is shoost now speakin' to a mob on de steps of de City Hall!"

The magnate did not wait to see me jump out of my chair or to hear my exclamations, but turned again to the telephone. "My Gawd, man! Vot do I know about it? De feller vas up in his room two hours ago ven we took him his dinner! He vouldn't eat it, he vouldn't speak—"

That was the last I heard, having bolted out of the room, and upstairs. I found Carpenter's door locked; I opened it, and rushed in. The place was empty! The bird had flown!

How had he got out? Had he climbed through the window and slid down a rain-spout in his prophetic robes? Had he won the heart of some servant? Had some newspaper reporter or agent of our enemies used bribery? I rushed downstairs, and got my car from the garage; and all the way to the city I spent my time in such futile speculations. How Carpenter, having escaped from the house, had managed to get into town so quickly—that was much easier to figure out; for our highways are full of motor traffic, and almost any driver will take in a stranger.

I came to the city. Even outside the crowded district, the traffic was held up for a minute or two at every corner; so I found time to look about, and to realize that the Brigade had got to town. All day special trains had been pouring into the city, literally dozens of them by every road; and now the streets were thronged with men in uniform, marching arm in arm, shouting, chanting war-cries, roaming in search of adventure. Tomorrow was the first day of the convention, the day of the big parade: tonight was a night of riot. Everything in town was free to ex-service men—and to all others who could borrow or buy a uniform. The spirit of the occasion was set forth in a notice published on the editorial page of the "Times":

"Hello, bo! Have a cigarette. Take another one. Take anything you see around the place.

"The town is yours. Take it into camp with you. Scruff it up to your heart's content. Order it about. Let it carry grub to you. Have it shine your shoes. Hand it your coat and tell it to hold it until the show is over.

"We are all waiting your orders. Shove us back if we crowd. Push us off the street. Give us your grip and tell us where to deliver it. Any errands? Call us. If you want to go anywhere, don't ask for directions. Just jump into the car and tell us where you're bound for.

"Let's have another one before we part. Put up your money; it's no good here. This one's on Western City."

I saw that it was not going to be possible to drive through the jam, so I put my car in a parking place, and set out for the City Hall on foot. On the way I observed that the invitation of the "Times" had been accepted; the Brigade had taken possession of the town. It was just about possible to walk on the down-town streets; there were solid masses of noisy, pushing people, every other man in uniform. Evidently there had been a tagit agreement to repeal the Eighteenth amendment to the Constitution for the next three days; bootleggers had drawn up their trucks and automobiles along the curbs, and corn-whiskey, otherwise known as "white lightnin'," was freely sold. You would meet a man with a bottle in his hand, and the effects of other bottles in his face, who would embrace you and offer you a drink; in the same block you would meet another man who would invite you to buy drinks for everybody in sight. The town had apparently agreed that no invitation should be declined. If the great Republic of Mobland had been unable to make for its returned war-heroes the new world which it had promised them—if it could not even give them back the jobs they had had before they left—surely the least it could do was to get them drunk!

And several times in each block you would have to get off the sidewalk for a group of ten or twenty flushed, dishevelled men, playing the great national game of craps. "Roll the bones!" they would shout, completely ignoring the throngs which surged about them. Each had his pile of bills and silver laid out on the pavement, and his bottle of "white lightnin';" now and then one would take a swig, and now and then one would start singing:

All we do is sign the pay-roll—
And we don't get a goddam cent.

You would go a little farther, and find a couple of automobiles trying to get past, and a merry crowd amusing itself throwing large waste cans in front of them. Some one would shout: "Who won the war?" And the answer would come booming: "The goddam slackers;" or maybe it would be, "The goddam officers." The crowd would move along, starting to chant the favorite refrain:

> You're in the army now,
> You're not behind the plow—;
> You son-of-a—,
> You'll never get rich—
> You're in the army now!

And from farther down the street would come a chorus from another crowd of marchers:

> I got a girl in Baltimore,
> The street-car runs right by her door.

Every now and then you would come on a fist-fight, or maybe a fight with bottles, and a crowd, laughing and whooping, engaged in pulling the warriors apart and sitting on them. Through a mile or two of this kind of thing I made my way, my heart sinking deeper with misgiving. I got within a couple of blocks of the City Hall, and then suddenly I came upon the thing I dreaded—my friend Carpenter in the hands of the mob!

LXI

THEY had got hold of a canvas-covered wagon, of the type of the old "prairie-schooner." You still find these camped by our roadsides now and then, with nomad families in them; and evidently one of these families had been so ill advised as to come to town for the convention. The rioters had hoisted their victim on top of the wagon, having first dumped a gallon of red paint over his head, so that everyone might know him for the Red Prophet they had been reading about in the papers. They had tied a long rope to the shaft of the wagon, and one or two hundred men had hold of it, and were hauling it through the streets, dancing and singing, shouting murder-threats against the "reds." Some ran ahead, to clear the traffic; and then came the wagon, lumbering and rocking, so that the prophet was thrown from side to side. Fortunately there was a hole in the canvas, and he could hold to one of the wooden ribs.

The cortege came opposite to me. On each side was a guard of honor, a line of men walking in lock-step, each with his hands on the shoulders of the one in front; they had got up a sort of chant: "Hi! Hi! The Bolsheviki prophet! Hi! Hi! The Bolsheviki prophet!" And others would yell, "I won't work! I won't work!"—this being our Mobland nickname for the I.W.W. Some one had daubed the letters on the sides of the wagon, using the red paint; and a drunken fellow standing near me shook his clenched fist at the wretch on top and bellowed in a fog-horn voice: "Hey, there, you goddam Arnychist, if you're a prophet, come down from that there wagon and cure my venereal disease!" There was a roar of laughter from the throng, and the drunken fellow liked the sensation so well that he walked alongside, shouting his challenge again and again.

Then I heard a crash behind me, and a clatter of falling glass; I turned to see a soldier, inside the Royal Hotel, engaged in chopping out the plate-glass window of the lobby with a chair. There were twenty or thirty uniformed men behind him, who wanted to get out and see the fun; but the door of the hotel was blocked by the crowd, so they were seeking a direct route to the goal of their desires.

I knew, of course, there was nothing I could do; one might as well have tried to stop a hurricane by blowing one's breath. Carpenter had wanted martyrdom, and now he was going to get it—of the peculiar kind and in the peculiar fashion of our free and independent and happy-go-lucky land. We have had many agitators and disturbers of our self-satisfaction, and they have all "got theirs," in one form or another; but there had never been one who had done quite so much to make himself odious as this "Bolsheviki prophet," who was now "getting his." "Treat 'em rough!" runs the formula of the army; and I fell in step, watching, and thinking that later I might serve as one of the stretcher-bearers.

Half way down the block we came to the Palace Hotel, and uniformed men came pouring out of that. I heard the shrieks of a woman, and put my foot on the edge of a store-window, and raised myself up by an awning, to see over the heads of the crowd. Half a dozen rowdies had got hold of a girl; I don't know what she had done—maybe her skirts were too short, or maybe she had been saucy to one of the gang; anyhow, they were tearing her clothes to shreds, and having done this gaily, they took her on their shoulders, and ran her out to the wagon, and tossed her up beside the Red Prophet. "There's a girl for you!" they yelled; and the drunken fellow who wanted Carpenter to cure him, suddenly thought of a new witticism: "Hey, you goddam Bolsheviki, why don't you nationalize her?" Men laughed and whooped over that; some of them were so tickled that they danced about and waved their arms in the air. For, you see, they knew all the details concerning the "nationalization of women in Russia," and also they had read in the papers about Mary Magna, and Carpenter's fondness for picture-actresses and other gay ladies. He stretched out his hand to the girl, to save her from falling off; and at this there went up such a roar from the mob, that it made me think of wild beasts in the arena. So to my whirling brain came back the words that Carpenter had spoken: "It is Rome! It is Rome! Rome that never dies!"

The cortege came to the "Hippodrome," which is our biggest theatre, and which, like everything else, had declared open house for Brigade members during the convention. Some one in the crowd evidently knew the building, and guided the procession down a side street, to the stage-entrance. They have all kinds of shows in the "Hippodrome," and have a driveway by which they bring in automobiles, or war-chariots, or wild animals in cages, or whatever they will. Now the mob stormed the entrance, and brushed the door-keepers to one side, and unbolted and swung back the big gates, and a swarm of yelling maniacs rushed the lumbering prairie-schooner up the slope into the building.

The unlucky girl rolled off at this point, and somebody caught her, and mercifully carried her to one side. The wagon rolled on; the advance guard swept everything out of the way, scenery as well as stage-hands and actors, and to the vast astonishment of an audience of a couple of thousand people, the long string of rope-pullers marched across the stage, and after them came the canvas-covered vehicle with the red-painted letters, and the red-painted victim clinging to the top. The khaki-clad swarm gathered about him, raising their deafening chant: "Hi! Hi! The Bolsheviki prophet. Hi! Hi! The Bolsheviki prophet!"

I had got near enough so that I could see what happened. I don't know whether Carpenter fainted; anyhow, he slipped from his perch, and a score of upraised hands caught him. Some one tore down a hanging from the walls of the stage set, and twenty or thirty men formed a cirfcle about it, and put the prophet in the middle of it, and began to toss him ten feet up into the air and catch him and throw him again.

And that was all I could stand—I turned and went out by the rear entrance of the theatre. The street in back was deserted; I stood there, with my hands clasped to my head, sick with disgust; I found myself repeating out loud, over and over again, those words of Carpenter: "It is Rome! It is Rome! Rome that never dies!"

A moment later I heard a crash of glass up above me; I ducked, just in time to avoid a shower of it. Then I looked up, and to my consternation saw the red-painted head and the red and white shoulders of Carpenter suddenly emerging. The shoulders were quickly followed by the rest of him; but fortunately there was a narrow shed between him and the ground. He struck the shed, and rolled, and as he fell, I caught him, and let him down without harm.

LXII

I expected to find my prophet nearly dead; I made ready to get him onto my shoulders and find some place to hide him. But to my surprise he started to his feet. I could not see much of him, because of the streams of paint; but I could see enough to realize that his face was contorted with fury. I remembered that gentle, compassionate countenance; never had I dreamed to see it like this!

He raised his clenched hands. "I meant to die for this people! But now—let them die for themselves!" And suddenly he reached out to me in a gesture of frenzy. "Let me get away from them! Anywhere, anyway! Let me go back where I was—where I do not see, where I do not hear, where I do not think! Let me go back to the church!"

With these words he started to run down the street; hauling up his long robes—never would I have dreamed that a prophet's bare legs could flash so quickly, that he could cover the ground at such amazing speed! I set out after him; I had stuck to him thus far, and meant to be in at the finish, whatever it was. We came out on Broadway again, and there were more crowds of soldier boys; the prophet sped past them, like a dog with a tin-can tied to its tail. He came to a cross-street, and dodged the crowded traffic, and I also got through, knocking pedestrians this way and that. People shouted, automobiles tooted; the soldiers whooped on the trail. I began to get short of breath, a little dizzy; the buildings seemed to rock before me, there were mobs everywhere, and hands clutching at me, nearly upsetting me. But still I followed my prophet with the bare flying legs; we swept around another corner, and I saw the goal to which the tormented soul was racing—St. Bartholomew's!

He went up the steps three at a time, and I went up four at a time behind him. He flung open the door and vanished inside; when I got in, he was half way up the aisle. I saw people in the church start up with cries of amazement; some grabbed me, but I broke away—and saw my prophet give three tremendous leaps. The first took him up the altar-steps; the second took him onto the altar; the third took him up into the stained-glass window.

And there he turned and faced me. His paint-smeared robes fell down about his bare legs, his convulsed and angry face became as gentle and compassionate as the paint would permit. With a wave of his hand, he signalled me to stand back and let him alone. Then the hand sank to his side, and he stood motionless. Exhausted, dizzy, I fell against one of the pews, and then into a seat, and bowed my head in my arms.

LXIII

I don't know just how much time passed after that. I felt a hand on my shoulder, and realized that some one was shaking me. I had a horror of hands reaching out for me, so I tried to get away from this one; but it persisted, and there was a voice, saying, "You must get up, my friend. It's time we closed. Are you ill?"

I raised my head; and first I glanced at the figure above the altar. It was perfectly motionless; and—incredible as it may seem—there was no trace of red paint upon either the face or the robes! The figure was dignified and serene, with a halo of light about its head—in short, it was the regulation stained glass figure that I had gazed at through all my childhood.

"What is the matter?" asked the voice at my side; and I looked up, and discovered the Reverend Mr. Simpkinson. He recognized me, and cried: "Why, Billy! For heaven sake, what has happened?"

I was dazed, and put my hand to my jaw. I realized that my head was aching, and that the place I touched was sore. "I—I—" I stammered. "Wait a minute." And then, "I think I was hurt." I tried to get my thoughts together. Had I been dreaming; and if so, how much was dream and how much was reality? "Tell me," I said, "is there a moving picture theatre near this church?"

"Why, yes," said he. "The Excelsior."

"And—was there some sort of riot?"

"Yes. Some ex-soldiers have been trying to keep people from going in there. They are still at it. You can hear them."

I listened. Yes, there was a murmur of voices outside. So I realized what had happened to me. I said: "I was in that mob, and I got beaten up. I was knocked pretty nearly silly, and fled in here."

"Dear me!" exclaimed the clergyman, his amiable face full of concern. He took me by my shoulders and helped me to my feet.

"I'm all right now," I said—"except that my jaw is swollen. Tell me, what time is it?"

"About six o'clock."

"For goodness sake!" I exclaimed. "I dreamed all that in an hour! I had the strangest dream—even now I can't make up my mind what was dream and what really happened." I thought for a moment. "Tell me, is there a convention of the Brigade—that is, I mean, of the American Legion in Western City now?"

"No," said the other; "at least, not that I've heard of. They've just held their big convention in Kansas City."

"Oh, I see! I remember—I read about it in the 'Nation.' They were pretty riotous—made a drunken orgy of it."

"Yes," said the clergyman. "I've heard that. It seems too bad."

"One thing more. Tell me, is there a picture of Mr. de Wiggs in the vestry-room?"

"Good gracious, no!" laughed the other. "Was that one of the things you dreamed? Maybe you're thinking of the portrait they are showing at the Academy."

"By George, that's it!" I said. "I patched the thing up out of all the people I know, and all the things I've read in the papers! I had been talking to a German critic, Dr. Henner—or wait a moment! Is he real? Yes, he came before I went to see the picture. He'll be entertained to hear about it. You see, the picture was supposed to be the delirium of a madman, and when I got this whack on the jaw, I set to work to have a delirium of my own, just as I had seen on the screen. It was the most amazing thing—so real, I mean. Every person I think of, I have to stop and make sure whether I really know them, or whether I dreamed them. Even you!"

"Was I in it?" laughed Mr. Simpkinson. "What did I do?"

But I decided I'd better not tell him. "It wasn't a polite dream," I said. "Let me see if I can walk now." I started down the aisle. "Yes, I'm all right."

"Do you suppose that crowd will bother you again? Perhaps I'd better go with you," said the apostle of muscular Christianity.

"No, no," I said. "They're not after me especially. I'll slip away in the other direction."

So I bade Mr. Simpkinson good-bye, and went out on the steps, and the fresh air felt good to me. I saw the crowd down the street; the ex-service men were still pushing and shouting, driving people away from the theatre. I stopped for one glance, then hurried away and turned the corner. As I was passing an office building, I saw a big limousine draw up. The door opened, and a woman stepped out: a bold, dark, vivid beauty, bedecked with jewels and gorgeous raiment of many sorts; a big black picture hat, with a flower garden and parts of an aviary on top—

Her glance lit on me. "My God! Will you look who's here!" She came to me with her two hands stretched out. "Billy, wretched creature, I haven't laid eyes on you for two months! Do you have to desert me entirely, just because you've fallen in love with a society girl with the face of a Japanese doll-baby? What's the matter with me, that I lose my lovers faster than I get them? I just met Edgerton Rosythe; he's got a good excuse, I admit—I'm almost as much scared of his wife as he is himself. But still, I'd like a chance to get tired of some man first! Want to come upstairs with me, and see what Planchet's doing to my old grannie in her scalping-shop? Say, would you think it would take three days' labor for half a dozen Sioux squaws to pull the skin off one old lady's back? And a week to tie up the corners of her mouth and give her a permanent smile! 'Why, grannie,' I said, 'good God, it would be cheaper to hire Charlie Chaplin to walk around in front of you all the rest of your life.' But the old girl was bound to be beautiful, so I said to Planchet, 'Make her new from the waist up, Madame, for you never can tell how the fashions'll change, and what she'll need to show.'"

And so I knew that I was back in the real world.

APPENDIX

WE live in an age, the first in human history, when religion is entirely excluded from politics and politics from religion. It may happen, therefore, that millions of men will read this story and think it merely a joke; not realizing that it is a literal translation of the life of the world's greatest revolutionary martyr, the founder of the world's first proletarian party. For the benefit of those whose historical education has been neglected, I append a series of references. The number to the left refers to a page of this book. The number to the right is a parallel reference to a volume of ancient records known as the Bible; specifically to those portions known as the gospels according to Matthew Everett, Mark Abell, Luka Korwsky, and John Colver.

```
11........Matthew 14:27
14........Matthew 6:21
16........Isaiah 3:16-26
17........Mark 12:37
70........Luke 6:24
70........John 15:17
72........Luke 9:38
73........Luke 4:40
75........Luke 11:46
78........Matthew 19:14
84........John 15:27
85........Luke 6:25
90........Matthew 12:39
95........Matthew 12:34
99........Matthew 10:9
102........Luke 4:5-8
107........Matthew 26:34
114........Matthew 26:69-75
117........James 5:1-6
119........Matthew 7:7
120........Matthew 7:11
123........Matthew 10:34
123........Matthew 10:16-17
129........Luke 23:23
131........Matthew 9:9
135........Acts 17:24
136........Matthew 21:12
136........Exodus 20:7
136........Matthew 21:13
138........Matthew 5:39-40
140........Matthew 23:1-33
143........Mark 6:56
```

143........Luke 6:19
144........Matthew 25:36
144........Matthew 21:6
145........Mark 3:20
145........Luke 5:29
146........Matthew 9:37
146........Luke 4:39
150........John 19:26
153........Matthew 19:16
155........Mark 15:14
162........Matthew 5:9
164........Luke 4:18
164........Luke 19:40-44
164........Matthew 11:5
167........Matthew 5:44
171........Matthew 27:14
171........Matthew 8:20
175........Matthew 26:7-13
176........Luke 1:52
179........Matthew 11:19
180........Matthew 5:11
182........Luke 20:20
182........Matthew 26:22
183........Matthew 26:36
185........John 18:3
186........Luke 22:4
190........Matthew 26:40
192........Luke 22:44
193........Matthew 26:40
194........Luke 14:43
195........Matthew 26:52
202........Mark 14:36
203........Matthew 10:28
214........Mark 15:18
214........Luke 23:38
214........Matthew 27:40

The Echo Library
www.echo-library.com

Please visit our website to download a complete catalogue of our books. We specialise in out-of-copyright reprints in all subjects. We publish a range of Large Print Editions of classic titles.

Books for re-printing

Suggestions for re-printing can be sent to titles@echo-library.com. Titles must be out-of-copyright or you must own the copyright. They can be in digital or published form.

If we do not wish to add the title to our catalogue then we can reprint for you. Costs depend on the format of the manuscript or book and its size.

Feedback

Because we have no direct contact with our customers we would welcome constructive comments to feedback@echo-library.com

Complaints

If there is a serious error in the text or layout please advise us by sending details to complaints@echo-library.com and we will supply a corrected copy, usually within 15 working days (it may take longer outside the UK and USA).

If there is a printing fault or the book is damaged please refer to your supplier.

CPSIA information can be obtained
at www.ICGtesting.com
Printed in the USA
LVOW03s1212191217
560231LV00001B/183/P